The Flow of Ashes and Virtue of Silence

Bernard Mparegh

The characters and events portrayed in this book are fictitious. Any similarity to real persons, living or dead, is coincidental and not intended by the author.

ISBN: 9789789769490

Cover design by: Mparegh Bernard Mveuter

DEDICATION

This book is dedicated to God Almighty, Mrs. Eunice E. Ortom, Ph.D for her giant steps in transforming the lives of less privileged indigens of Benue State through her Pet Project, "The Eunice Spring of Life Foundation," and to my Elder brother Mparegh Benjamin Kamimi.

FOREWORD

"The flow of ashes" epitomizes the power of fate and destiny, hard-work and determination, resilience and steadfastness against all odds. The immediate circle of societal issues revolves around this tale. It is an eye opener to critical minds touring the planes of life without a stable condition of comfort. Indeed, silence is a virtue and the virtue of silence expose the other side of the semantics. This elegant piece dwells on the marriage and family life. It highlights on infidelity and gentility, throwing open the doors of relationships and their attendant complexities. It is one piece sure to keep you on the edge of your seat. Rev.fr.dr. Didacus kajo (ksm) federal university of agriculture makurdi benue state, nigeria. May, 2019.

PREFACE

The flow of ashes many people's destinies have been caged or possibly denied right from childhood by some so called guardians. They would experience a lot of misfortune as a result and properly suffer from inferiority complex. These same wicked guardians clamor round the clock to better the lives of their biological children. By so doing they deprive the less privileged or orphans under them from getting the best or getting higher, totally harboring partiality and lack of love, forgetting the emblems of the flow of ashes for nature. The author has carefully mirrored the society using the works of ashes as it flies back to the one that throws it away. This signifies that whatever done to other human turns back, be it good or bad. The author has made an effort in the African style of writing to morally inform the society about love, impartiality, justice, kindness, honesty and peace, so as to awaken the minds that are still held captive in immoral deeds to decede from them for the betterment of the society.

Virtue of silence

Silence is a virtue that needs to be much

considered because of its power. It turns out to be the least in the life of many individuals now in the society and its negligence has been drastically reducing cordial relationships, breaking marriages, organizations, institutions and what have you. Many people think that every situation is handled with force, power and authority, forgetting that silence most times settles problems and possibly terminate their occurrences. But we can far better understand how to settle problems and some situations peacefully when we try to kill mosquitoes on testes. In the novel the character; tako keghnen had used the virtue to settle a situation which gallons of holy water won't have made a way. Always remember the virtue of silence and you'll be an icon. Mparegh bernard mveuter april, 2019.

CONTENTS

ACKNOWLEDGMENTS

I wish to acknowledge the following humble individuals for their contributions towards the successful production of this work. But first and foremost my gratitude goes to God Almighty for giving me the opportunity to put this idea on paper. To Prof. Utim Ate, Dr.Mrs. Eunice E. Ortom, Chief. Dr. Terkura Suswam, Rev. Fr. Dr. Didacus Kajo, and Dr. Iveren Chenge, I whole heartedly appreciate your support for the success of this work may God continue to bless you. Never to forget the array of heads that committed to this work, Dr. S.T. Wuese, Comr. Moses T. Ayange, and Comr. Tiza Geoffrey. I sincerely acknowledge your tireless works on the edition of this book, may the source of your generosities never be dried. To my parents, the best that could ever be found on earth; Mr. & Mrs. John Saaulu Mparegh for their sponsorship and encouragement for the success of this work. Of course my brothers; Mparegh Benjamin Kamimi, Mparegh Boniface Saater, Mparegh Barnabas Sesughter and my sister Mparegh Ngohile, for everything you did to bring the raw manuscript to the current state I am eternally indebted. To Sir Kase Christopher Kase and Mbaiorga Kehen, I sincerely appreciate your patience and endurance on your computer for the success of this work. Sir, I'm grateful. I extend my gratitude also to my wonderful teachers at Gift Nur/Primary School Gboko East, Uplift Secondary School Gboko, Madona High School Iorza, Logo Local Government Area, Government Day Secondary School Buter, Gboko North and to my loving lecturers at the Federal University of Agriculture Makurdi especially the ones in the Department of Forestry. Your efforts are seen. To Moses Mbaiorga, Ger Torkuma, Sheila Timothy Ede-Abel, Akor Stephen, Peter Tor, and Gabriel Daper. You are wonderful Finally to all my numerous friends, mates from all the schools I have attended, whom the pressure of time and space has made impossible for me to mention here you are highly appreciated.

THE FLOW OF ASHES

I

It was not up to an hour after the heavy rain had stopped, the birds huddled together in clusters for warmth. The smile of the gentle cloud created space delightedly as the sun emerged happily, being on duty again. It was in the morning when the pregnant cloud gave birth. Since the day was still young and agile, the sun reappeared for its daily duty. Little breeze whispered through some beautiful and proudly freshen flowers compatibly planted in Excellence International High School Makurdi making the school environment more cold and tranquil like a graveyard, as if the school was on a holiday where only a pyramid of lifeless desks could be seen-motionless and speechless. The rain seemed odd for the little ones, because since two decades ago such rain had not been experienced. Then, the rainy season would start early in the year around April and stop normally in late October like a tradition in West Africa, precisely Nigeria; a humid sub-tropical region, and very productive, which all farmers cherished most for agricultural practices. The rainy season would begin with a heavy rain that starts with the darkening of the sky in the Northern part of the country and with a whirl wind that influences a thick dust to dance fiercely in the atmosphere, making it difficult for someone to see the sky clearly. Weightless objects like leaves and waterproof would whirl in the wind and disappear into the sky. It would start with some stony precipitate and subsequently, the real heavy rain would kick-off. When it rains in torrents and thunder clapping accompanied by lightening, the farmers would jubilate in anticipation of a bumper harvest during harvest time. But adversely, there would be lots of destruction and at times loss of lives would be recorded. Gboko; the central home of the Tiv people once received its fair share of one of such destructive rains; the damage was colossal and monumental as many houses were affected. Buildings collapsed, roofs were blown open, mighty and small trees fell, blocking high ways and houses built in lowland areas flooded. People watched at the affected places like in cinema in disbelief. The victims and other inhabitants inconvincibly wished to have built in deserts or rather mountains than staying without safety. Many terrible things were experienced by the heavy rain. It had happened again which seemed unusual to the little ones as compared to the normal drizzling rain they had experienced over the years; while the adults were amazed and they marveled speechlessly for experiencing such a heavy rain again. Shortly, the school bell rang for closure and the students shouted with joy in expression of happiness as they were dismissed. They piled up their notebooks as fast as they could. It seemed they longed for dismissal like the second coming of Christ. It was an astute move for those of them who took their cardigan. It aided them to cover themselves in the cold weather while others who were shivering and gnashing their teeth were those who wore only school uniform of pure white up and black down which would make students of other institutions admire them. Some were rushing to their hostels while others were walking out of the school gate to go home. Excellence International High School was a day and boarding school located at plot 2 Kings Way, Lords' Crescent in Makurdi. It covered the area of 8sq.km; about four buildings of the school were built in two storey buildings, well painted with a dark yellow colour to suit the green roofed slate, well electrified with lots of beautiful flowers surrounding them. The male and female hostels were demarcated with the security block, which was adjacent to the computer classes where students received their computer lessons all the times. The football field and some other courts were well constructed; the masquerade tree called Polyathia longifolia was planted on every walk way, giving each a distance of about ten feet. Also, some vital trees that could provide enough shade for relaxation were planted. The environment was conducive. By viewing, it was indeed a small New York as the town boys would reckon it. The School was academically sound with well disciplined and professional teachers. It was founded by a politician who came back from Canada, with a great zeal of enlightening his people through education. For that reason, he made it day and boarding so that parents who needs sound education for their ward could have access. The school fee as well was much affordable for almost every parent. Mdoo, was a senior student, a very beautiful girl with bulge eyes completely white and charming, pointed nose and black polished hairs on her head. She was tall, slim and chocolate complexioned. A lady any sane man would describe as an epitome of beauty. She was a science student in SSS 3A. Very brilliant, she was then the outgoing head girl of the school. She was so much loved by the students for her love and concern for them. She abruptly stood by the sound of the closing bell and piled some text books on her desk in the library from the Readers' Department and took them along with her borrower's ticket for charge. Senior School Certificate Examinations (SSCE) was fast approaching and she was getting more and more serious with her studies. She was always in the library reading especially during free periods.

Mdoo would make sure that none of her precious time was spent out in vain. She proceeded to her class to pick her school bag; she slung it on her shoulders and headed to Afa's class when a familiar voice called in front of her. She stretched her eyes not letting her eyelid blink, while her forehead winkled as to see clearly who had called her. "Oh it is Sir Jackson!" she exclaimed. But rather relieved, "What could be the matter?" she pursued rhetorically under her breath. Sir Jackson was a fair handsome young man of early thirties about 6 feet tall. He liked dressing in white with a black panama hat always covered on his head. He had the same dress code compared to that of the world known great musician; Michael Jackson, thus students nick named him "Sir Jackson". He was Mdoo's chemistry teacher, very intelligent, a real bookman who spent some years in Canada. Students often wondered why he was not a lecturer in one of the universities in Nigeria, than teaching in a secondary school. Perhaps there might be some connections between him and the proprietor since both of them had been to Canada, or possibly, he was for a contract and some day he would return back. But that, he had not once talked about it and it threw his students into confusion but none of them had gotten the courage to ask him. That was the belief some students had, that such men were supposed not to have been teaching in the secondary schools but in higher institutions. His spoken English was similar to the whites, the reason why most students were fond of him. Whenever he spoke, they would snort with laughter. They loved imitating him with his pronunciation of words. His generosity was immeasurable. In the students cycle of contention they believed his exposure was responsible for his joviality. He stood with his hand clamped on the staff Common-room door and his head stooped forward indicating his greater height for the door. He looked smart and agile. "Good afternoon sir" Mdoo greeted and genuflected as she reached where her tutor stood. He was pleased with her attitude, he gave a smile and reiterated with gesture "Good afternoon head, girl how are you?" Mdoo managed between laughter, but finally burst in when she heard her teacher feigning a feminine voice. "I am fine sir." Mdoo replied. "The principal would want to see you before you leave." He softly said but now rather sincere. "Okay thank you sir" "Good! Have a nice weekend" he said and then got back to the staff common-room. "The principal…?" Mdoo muttered under her breathe as she turned for the principal's office. "What could be the matter when the bell had already been rang?" she questioned herself moving towards the principal's office. It was strange for her because since she was admitted into the school she had not for once been called to the principal's office. Her admission was conducted in the vice principal's office, her prefectship interview was also in the vice principal's office and whenever there was a call for a quiz competition it would be the vice principal who would conduct it. The principal would only talk to his students on the assembly ground and in their classes as the case may be, he had not for once called any of his students to his office or asked them to tidy it up, only for a reason best known to him. He had his cleaner who took care of his office. But today Sir Jackson had informed Mdoo that her attention was needed in the principal's office, a situation that threw Mdoo in a sea of confusion. She seemed confused and couldn't compose herself as it was odd for her. She kept asking rhetorically "Have I done anything wrong? No but if yes of what magnitude has it reached for the principal to request my presence in his office? Or would it be Afa? Has she fought anyone again? Or has she insulted anyone? I doubt, anyway, let me get there first." She thought intensively as it firmly gripped her heart, but at the same time she tried to bury the issue of such an urgent call from the principal because of its effects as to occupy it with something else. "Ha! Afa would be looking for me." She muttered again to herself as she kept her eyes peeled for

Afa but could not clap her eyes on her. She could not succeed the dominance of it and she deliberated over it again. It was not too long that she got interrupted as she stepped her feet on the principal's corridor. The corridor was built some inches high with some climbing steps on every office door on the block. Mdoo had climbed the steps now facing the principal's office door. By her left it was the office of the vice principal admin and by her right was the office of the vice principal academics with inscriptions boldly written on various offices. They were all closed indicating they had all gone for the weekend. A neat white and green curtain designed in form of the Nigerian flag was hanged on the principal's office door, taking exactly the size and height of the office door. The wind blew and the curtain flinched a little. Mdoo had managed to peer through, she saw the principal. And then her heart began to jump. She was not really expecting his absence for she was well told that the principal was in the office. But she could not actually explain what caused her unusual heart beat. The principal hardly stays in school by this time; Mdoo thought again. She gave a deep sigh to restore her equanimity, now it was better off. "Sir may I come in?" Mdoo said with a trembling voice. "Yes come in" the principal permitted. He was a fat and tall man with a big hooked nose and a cop voice full of confidence. Mdoo would wonder whether his fatness was responsible for such confidence. Mdoo walked in, anxious perhaps to hear reprimanding words from the principal like on your knees. She stood in the door way. The principal raised on her, his two set of eyes that nearly pushed off his transparent specs with a blink of his red eyes inside the glasses like the sudden blink of the traffic warning light. "Yes!" the principal exclaimed, wearing away his anticipation. "Good afternoon sir" Mdoo greeted. "Good afternoon head girl, how are you?" "I am… am… fine sir." She answered with an unsteady voice. If not for the Principal, Mdoo had not noticed the presence of the man in the principal's office as their conversation ceased on her arrival. She was surprised and immediately bent apologetically as she greeted him letting him to know she did not see him also as a result of the weather that made the office dim even as the curtains were pulled up. He was an aged man, a bit tall and dressed in suit. He looked very responsible. In his appearance, he must be a rich man, Mdoo had thought. The principal and the man resumed their conversation about the less seriousness of students relating to the effects it has on the society as well as the numerous social vices caused by some drop outs and those who deliberately refused to go to school. They also pointed out those that walk up and down the streets smoking, injecting, swallowing and inhaling hard drugs, thereby availing themselves as instruments of thuggery used by some devious politicians for their political ambitions. The principal was so much enthusiastic in the discussion that he almost forgot Mdoo's issue. She sat quietly facing them nervously like a long-tailed cat in a room full of rocking chairs. She stared around at the walls of the office and her eyes lingered on the calendars of the school occasions. She kept starring at each of them. She recognized herself in one of the calendars that was suspended on the wall. She stood with the principal, teachers and other students. In another direction were some golden cups placed on a very high table, she had also recognized those golden cups very well. She was the one that won those golden cups for six consecutive competitions conducted in the state. She could not recall all the competitions she and some students had participated and won for the school. Mdoo had also remembered the school generator which was also won by her. She had won many prizes for the school and for herself. If one could talk about a brilliant person, Mdoo was a good example. She was so intelligent. Mdoo admired the beauty of the office and wished for something like that in her future. The office was well rugged with executive chairs round and a glass stool placed by the right side at each of the chairs. A steel shelf was there filled with encyclopedias, journals, newspapers, novels and copies of the school magazines and prospectus. A white small refrigerator was also placed at the principal's right hand side. She had imagined the amount of money that was spent on the office. The more she stared around, the better she admired. "No wonder the principal is always looking fresh like bankers," she had discovered the secret. She was only taken back when she heard the principal's voice descending. "Head girl," the principal called drawing her attention to what he was about to say. "Sir!" Mdoo answered quickly. "This is my best friend he is the personal assistant to the commissioner of education. He was my classmate back then in the primary school. We were discussing and I was telling him about you and showing him the prizes you have won for the school in as much as many students had decided to be so lackadaisical about their studies and he requested to see you. That was why I sent for you." After the principal had said this, a smile aroused at Mdoo's face showing a little gesture of excitement to his statement. "Head girl how are you doing?" the principal's friend asked as he jolted from the sofa. "I am fine sir" Mdoo answered. "Your principal told me a lot about your performances and I must confess you are a genius". Mdoo needed no one to explain to her that it was a warm compliment but accepting it with a verbal response was the challenge, rather she stoop her head down her chest with a smile and the man continued, "I just wanted to see you and then encourage you to do more. Endeavor not to relent okay, being serious with your academics has been the best decision you have made." "Thank you sir" Mdoo appreciated as he finally landed. These words were not new to her; she had heard them repeatedly from Agwaza. He would say them to her time without number which she believed only a kind person would use them on someone, thus it made her thought of him to be a good man. The man took a brief case he had dropped on the glass stool beside him and brought out some pieces of one thousand naira unit notes. "My dear have this" he said and handed over the money to Mdoo repositioning himself on the sofa. Mdoo was very surprised and filled with joy. The principal seemed much more surprise than Mdoo the recipient. Mdoo received the money with trembling hands. The principal collected the money from Mdoo and enveloped it and gave it back to her. Suddenly, happiness filled her body like a bomb explosion and she experienced an impulsive perspiration that spread all over her brow. It was a surprise to have experienced it in such inclement. Joy engulfed her, she was giddy with happiness. It drove off her words, all she could say was "Thank you sir" with a radiant smile. "It's okay, let's thank God" the man happily said. Mdoo was over excited. The spirit of happiness in her was great. Excitement dragged Mdoo out of the principal's office as if she was pushed off or chased out by someone. She jumped down the corridor skipping the steps with a plastered smile. She heard a horror shriek at her back. It was Afa Agwaza who hid beside the block. "Oh Afa how did you know I am here?" Mdoo asked surprisingly. "I saw you when you were heading towards the principal's office" Afa replied. "Sorry to have kept you waiting" Mdoo pleaded. "No...No... come-on, there is no problem. You are the Head girl I understand how your work is stressful. Besides, it's the principal that sent for you". "Oh! Thank you my dear" Mdoo said giving her a hug worth her patient mind exhibited earlier. Mdoo you look very excited, any secret?" Afa asked noticing the joy that was written all over Mdoo. "Very obvious, come on Afa guess" "Okay fine, the SSCE time table is out" Afa presumed, for she thought anything that could make Mdoo so exhilarated was only something that related with her academics. "No you missed it" "So what's it?" "Afa, think and guess again..." "Ooh... that's what I can only fetch" "Alright, no more stress, Afa, I have been given some money by the principal's friend who is the personal assistant to the commissioner of education." "Just like that?" Afa asked expressing some little confusion. "Just like that, he is still in the principal's office" "You don't mean it!" Afa exclaimed in surprise. "Hmm" Mdoo grunted and pulled down the zip on her school bag very little and pushed out some notes out of the envelope that the principal had given to her. Afa did not miss the sight of it "uwuu!" she exclaimed with her palm clapping on her mouth "Waoh! This is great. No... No... lets go home, Daddy and Mummy must hear this" she said in excitement and patted Mdoo's arms. They quickly walked with short unsteady steps out of the school premises like children who had recently learnt how to walk. They were indeed excited. They were day students although, their sponsor; Agwaza had enough money to pay for boarding but he did not like the idea. If only Mr. Dickson had disclosed his intension of giving such money to Mdoo the principal would have preferred the assembly ground to boost other student's morale. Notwithstanding, he would definitely announce it on Monday. For sure he was not going to leave it mute. Next Monday was there, he was going to stand before the students on the assembly ground with his serious face fixed on them and his left hand in the pocket and students would sense it that yes he was yet for another serious matter. Then he would call Mdoo out to the students as usual to tell them the offer that Mdoo had received from his friend, the Personal Assistance to the Commissioner of Education, only because he had spoken with him about her performances. And then he would finally encourage them to be more serious with their academics. Although there were some other intellectuals and many who were averagely good but Mdoo was their grand tutor.

II

The streets were heavily congested with all manners of vehicles. Lots of hawkers were making signs for notice. Mini-bus drivers and their conductors were hailing for passengers and the wheelbarrow pushers piled up around the buses to offload and then load goods of alighting passengers. Keke-NAPEP drivers were dangling like lunatics drawing circles. Mini-bus drivers sometimes would make one believe they were born with those activities. It was so easy for strangers to get confused and miss their way with their sharp pronunciation and whistling of places in hurry. They would call North-Bank to everyone's hearing as Nol ban and they would call Brewery and Gaadi route of Makurdi as Brega Brega. They would make the town filled, hustled and busted. They were indeed real in fulfilling the biblical injunction of "no food for lazy man". Mdoo felt running home would be faster than using a motorcycle. The motorcycle they climbed was not moving as fast as she expected. She wished aircrafts were available and able to give door to door services. She seemed madly in thought but what could nature have over such happiness. Mdoo's guardian, Agwaza Bunde was an Engineer in his mid-fifties with Shabu-Bidi Cement

Industry in Makurdi. He was not too wealthy but had enough to take care of his family and was a God-fearing man. Tall and dark with an athletic figure, he had a bald head very glittery like a dazzling glass in the sun. Afa his daughter, when growing up would mischievously gaze at it as to see whether there would be a reflection of her image. He had a pointed nose that was exactly as that of Mdoo. Hence Fridays were early closing days from many places of work especially in academics which had been enacted into law. He sat outside the house with his back leaned on a wooden arm chair reading a magazine by the Star Times under a shade. And with him was his pretty wife; Ngodoo who hardly smiled. She sat and was fixing and painting her artificial nails in design, while the whispering breeze after the rain set both of them comfortable in the environment. Agwaza loved Mdoo very much; her behaviors were what Agwaza would want someone to have. Her brilliancy and assiduousness were what really thrilled him. But his wife was contradictory, she had no affection on whatever Mdoo did, her reason being that, Mdoo was not her biological daughter. She had complained without response from Agwaza on several occasions over loving Mdoo more than Afa his biological daughter. Thus, her hatred over Mdoo increased with each passing day. Little after, Mdoo and Afa stormed the house like a raving wolf chasing its prey or like those who were being chased by mad dogs. Agwaza and his wife watched in perplexity as the girls toddle with excitement towards them. Agwaza stared curiously, expecting from them the cause of their happiness. Mdoo fasten her feet to where Agwaza sat. "Daddy the Lord has done it again" she shrieked excitedly. Agwaza and his wife's eyes popped out as Mdoo brought out the envelope from her school bag, in unison Agwaza and his wife imagined of what magnitude would be the cause of such happiness from the girls. "Daddy this was given to me by the principal's friend; the Personal Assistant to the Commissioner of Education who came to visit him. The principal sent for me that the man wanted to see me. According to the man, the principal had told him about me while in their discussion that was why he wanted to see me and then he gave me this." After she finished, she then handed the envelope to Agwaza. Agwaza was surprised to have seen the content of the envelope. "What!" He exclaimed. Mdoo won't stop surprising him; day after day she was surprising him. He felt happy and became dumbfounded. He suddenly stared around in a moment and then became fixed on Afa as if to say; Afa have you seen what seriousness could do? Can you see what diligence could do? More favours await such a person in life. Ngodoo became furious she wrinkled her nose in disgust and swirled her eyeball aggressively. Mdoo did not miss the sight, Ngodoo felt uneasy sitting, and she sat sulking, for she had nothing to do in Agwaza's presence for she knew well that Agwaza would not take any mess from her. Agwaza embraced Mdoo and called out for celebration. Agwaza would question himself rhetorically why Mdoo resembled him more than Afa his biological daughter. Indeed she resembled Agwaza if not for the beautiful womanly figure Mdoo had that was exceptional, yet her nose was as that of Agwaza. What a coincidence!

III

Two days had passed after Mdoo had written her Joint Admission and Matriculation Examination (JAMB). Unlike years back when Jamb would be written and one had to wait for scores for weeks. This time around, it wasn't like that. Few hours after writing, your scores would be sent to your telephone number which you used during registration process. Mdoo's result was yet to be out like other students had written on the same day and time with her. Whenever she became worried, her guardian would always give her assurances never to worry. That was her first time of writing an examination on a computer, although she was acquainted to computers. She had also complained much about the running seconds of the computer when she was answering her questions and now why the delay of the result. She was bothered much on what would be her scores, whether she would make up the minimum points or not. Each time she thought of that she would console herself with the words "failure is never my portion". Ngodoo was very happy with the situation at hand. She wished Mdoo failed the examination so that her husband would for once be disappointed with her just the same way he was when Afa failed so that the chorus of "Mdoo is a brilliant girl" would end at least for once or fade. It was on the fifth day after Mdoo wrote the exams. She was in the sitting room when she received an SMS from JAMB revealing her scores to be 290. She was flabbergasted dumbfounded, and shouted out "Jesus". She was overwhelmed. This is miraculous, she said. She had never thought of the scores she had gotten. She could not remember when she started singing praises to the lord, her joy was great. Her words of "my redeemer lives success is not optional" had now come to confirmation. It was so marvelous. Agwaza was not at home, he had gone out with a friend; by the time he returns great news await him. Mdoo would not stop surprising him; there it goes, here it comes again, life of a genius. The drum has been played it was now left for Ngodoo to decide whether to dance with bitter kola in her mouth or not. She was greatly annoyed by the news. All Agwaza could do was to congratulate Mdoo for he was lost for words.

IV

After four months, Mdoo had written the West African Examination council (WAEC) and National Examination council (NECO) Exams. Her graduation ceremony was by the corner. Days were running fast to the date of the graduation ceremony; running fast like the time Mdoo beheld on the day of her JAMB examination, it ran as though one was after it. The days had faithfully dragged by and clocked the D day. The day that was much expected by students had now arrived. It had always been during the period yearly but all the times students would wait anxiously for it. Without waste of time, Mdoo had finished dressing up, well prepared to leave with Agwaza and Afa for her graduation ceremony. Agwaza took permission from his work place, no need for one to tell him stories about such a blissful day of Mdoo; no... no live and direct he was going to witness it. No one earth could describe such an event to his satisfaction. This was the day for Agwaza to see Mdoo pass out in grand style. Meanwhile Ngodoo was not around, she had intentionally travelled two days before the D-day. Preparations were made to make the event a memorable one and to cheer up dignitaries. Besides it had been a tradition of Excellence International High School Makurdi to thrill their guests on such occasions. Agwaza, Mdoo and Afa had now arrived. Agwaza was ushered to a seat in the canopies where parents and guardians were seated. It was separated from other invited guests. Mdoo joined her fellow graduating students, while Afa was hanging around with her friends. The proprietor, being a politician had invited many dignitaries from all walks of life. The then Governor of the state who was his close friend sent a representative, the Commissioner of Education of the state was also present with his Personal Assistant; the principal's friend and other commissioners, four high ranking military officers were also present with their securities surrounded, only to mention but a few. Many people came because of the nature of the school environment and some because of the presence of the dignitaries. Indeed, it was a great occasion. Everything was well organized. Not long, activities commenced. The graduating students matched with their academic gowns to the canopy that was arranged for them. It started with an opening prayer led by a priest. Then the principal stood up and gave his welcome address which also covered all the achievements made by the school in the preceding session. He encouraged his students, both the graduating and the non-graduating students to be more serious and keep their candles burning. Thereafter, the guest speaker presented his speech, followed by the chairman of the occasion, the chairlady, the Commissioner of Education, the outgoing Head boy and Head girl also presented their speeches then the Governor and finally the proprietor. The school cultural troupe performed the Tiv, Idoma, Igbo, Hausa and Yoruba dances to thrill the guests. This was greeted with spreading of currencies by the elated guests. Next was the turn of drama and debate. When drama and debate were over, gifts were presented. Mdoo was the best graduating student. People were amazed and started pointing fingers at Agwaza as he made way for Mdoo to receive gifts. Mdoo received 11 gifts; best in 6 subjects, morals, neatness, in debate, as an overall best, and as an icon of the school. People ran short of words as the girl outshined other students to that limit. The Commissioner later stood again with an approval and called Mdoo out for a scholarship to study from undergraduate degree to PhD level in any university of her choice within the country. Hot tears streamed down from Agwaza's eyes to his chin. He dabbed his eyes with a handkerchief severally. People had seen what was meant by tears of joy. Mdoo had given it to him in fullness. Many dignitaries appreciated Mdoo's performances in monetary form, including the Personal Assistant to the Commissioner of Education; who had once given her twenty thousand naira. Two months after her graduation, her SSCE results were released with distinctions in all subjects. She was offered admission at the prestigious Benue State University, to study Medicine and Surgery. After Two years, Afa joined her in the same university to study Theatre Arts, the course of her choice.

V

At the University, the lifestyle of students was different compared to what Mdoo had imagined it to be. She had come to realize what campus life was all about. Hence no one would question another, no one would be chastised over his or her misdemeanors, and students were living their lives the way they wanted. Though some were living a much disciplined life, but those with bad behaviors seemed to be in the majority. She wondered why the university campus had no strict dos and don'ts. To her utmost dismay, sleazy things that were seen as taboos became the order of the day and plain fashions on campus in the name of school runs. Indecent dressing was their priority. She would see the female ones wearing what they called; no-bending, cross-no-gutter; short skirts far above the knees, and the male ones would sag torn trousers like mad men. She always wondered how they defined life. She wondered what they would become in future, and what they shall tell their future children. She also imagined how their parents would feel seeing them in such dreadful acts. She again, wondered what their purpose of coming to school was. "It is a shame for students who take no pity on their sponsors, after spending lots of hard-earned money for them to grab the cobwebs off their bright future, and even for the betterment of their unborn children; still they would not want to see it. What heartless students! What ingratitude!" Mdoo had once said to herself. What Mdoo used to experience at night, the day time was simply holy hours. Whenever the skies started wearing darkness, she would see wealthy men and women coming to pick the opposite sex in their flashy cars. She would see group of cultists attacking their rivals, butchering themselves like wild animals. They would harass innocent ladies; abuse them by rape, stealing and all manner of things they imagine to do in the name of protecting the supremacy of their confraternity. Mdoo was always feeling bad about campus life. But what could she do apart from preaching the good news of God to them? Abiding by God's words was Mdoo's priority. Agwaza's words also were always a mirror of reflection to her. She was just the opposite of a chameleon that changes its colour according to its surroundings for the reason of adaptation. Nothing about Mdoo's behavior had changed. Rather she was now burning more candles compared to her secondary school days. She was called Jackometer by her fellow mates. She was also known for TDB; Till Day Break kind of reading which seemed odd in the university. She had a friend; called Shimana whom they were morally and academically compatible. She was a dark beautiful lady, tall, slim but had a well formed body. She had a pointed nose, gleaming eyes that always set men in sight of her ablaze, and with black polished thick hair. Everything about her was indeed exquisite. Many men had knocked their heads, bit their fingers and wished to have her as house wife. Princess Shimana came from a family of two, she was the last born and only daughter of king Jorguno; the king of Mbaterem district. His Royal Highness Jorguno was a vibrant and happy king with good leadership qualities. He served his people with sufficient humility as a leader. He became depressed, after the irreparable loss of his beloved wife. Five years after he was crowned a king, she died in a ghastly motor accident on her way to an Organizational meeting with her driver. Her death was like a fist right in their eyes. A home that was filled with much joy and laughter, tragedy broke in once and made it as quiet as a grave yard; a forest was a good example to describe the state of the house. Her death was indeed a vacuum in their lives. Life is just nothing, when it is in you it is in you that's all of it. It is like a balloon filled with air anytime it decides it busts. It had now created a barrel of sorrows in a home of joy and left it loose. Death turned the once vibrant king to a king of emotions. Now how won't he be out of his mind when the recrudescence of how the villagers gossiped that he killed his wife kept appearing minute after minute! What a wicked world! When one losses a beloved one and is labeled as the killer, what a heartless people! Mdoo and Shimana loved each other like the love of a mother and her child. They were friends that cared for each other selflessly, friends with the same values of life. Friends that had like minds, they saw no fault in each other. They were true friends; their friendship was what everyone would admire, the most illuminative style in them that admirers cherished most was their sacrificial life for one another, always eager to sacrifice. They were not seen among the categories of those who did bad things on campus. Afa was different; she was not always reading her books. She preferred chasing campus life here and there and refused to take advice from anyone. She was becoming more obstinate as a mule. "Education is not my problem" she had often said. All her lectures then were centered at Akperan Orshi auditorium which was one of the largest auditoria on campus accommodating more than a thousand and eight hundred students, but normally a seating capacity of one thousand five hundred. She was fond of coming late to lectures and always seen at the last backseats where naughty and disruptive students often arranged themselves like huddled bees. She cared less. "How can an exquisite lady like me struggle for studies? Impossible! After all I have my perfect ways of awakening a sleeping lion. I cannot enslave myself to studies, certificate is certificate." These were her warm-up thoughts whenever she seemed lackadaisical for her education. But never did she think of how a good and defendable certificate could climb one high and how reputable it is in the society. She was getting worse every day. Whenever Mdoo tried to confront her over her bad attitudes, "please...please... save your unsolicited advice" would be her response or would end up walking out of Mdoo if she seemed not discouraged by her response. Mdoo now needed no soothsayer to squat down and cast sooth for her before she could tell what it was. Afa had been fed with reasons to hate her to the core. For only two years she had spent in school without Afa, she had a great change in her lifestyle; her mother had blended it well.

VI

Shimana had laughed out loud in the sitting room, it was Mdoo who had visited her. They sat to discuss about university experience relating it to their different secondary school experiences. Indeed secondary school days are unforgotten days, days when one would tell of his or her future ambition, how he or she will study medicine to become a medical doctor, study law to become a lawyer, study engineering to become an engineer and so on. They would study mighty courses as they would call in advance to become wonderful men and women in the society. And at times they would end up not studying what they have dreamt for, just a few that their ambition would be a true revelation of God's plan for their lives. Mdoo remembered her classmate Terdoo who once said he was going to study medicine and surgery at the university; he would mock and insult people who went to polytechnics, colleges of education, he would laugh at the courses they study. But he was now studying in the polytechnic. No one ever believed he would study there. It is indeed true when people say your life might not go the way you plan but the way God planned. Not a single course of study is inessential or infinitesimal in the society. Every course has its valuable function to make life whole. It also rang a bell in Mdoo's mind of a man who was being mocked by many people for his course while in the university. He became a millionaire with his certificate of the so called useless course. He became the saviour to those who once made mockery of him. They would come in clusters asking him to lend them money, and some would even come with rolling tears that without his help they would die of their predicaments. This was a good moment for them. They like to have times like this. Little later a man walked in. "Good day my dear you are welcome," Shimana greeted as she stood on her feet. "Good day sir" Mdoo joined in. "Good day ladies, how are you doing?" "Fine" they all chorused. "Mdoo meet my brother whom I told you about few days back." The princess said with her hand extending towards her brother, Kamimi. "Alright" "My prince this is Mdoo a good friend of mine" Shimana introduced Mdoo to Kamimi. He gave Mdoo a warm and infectious smile like a baby does on seeing the mother. "Nice to meet you" he stretched out his hand but Mdoo stood up from her sit and half bent before him and he turned his right hand and patted her arm gently. "Oh I can see you ladies are almost drenched with excitement" "Yeah exactly" "Waoh that's good, it's only that am jealous of you" the prince said and they all burst into laughter and he walked out gently leaving them in the sitting room. By now Mdoo was in four hundred level with her friend Shimana while Afa in two hundred level. She had now fully grown into a woman.

VII

As days rolled by, Kamimi seemed disturbed and weak, hour after hour like lazy students who are informed of an examination. Last night he could not sleep peacefully. Every single minute of sleep had a second of thought. About 12:45am he fully jacked up and leaned back at the edge of his room when there was silence everywhere. The only sound was that of the wall clock slowly ticking away seconds and the innocent rotation of the ceiling fan. He stared confused at each of them as if to say; you stop ticking and you no more rotate, let there be absolute silence. But the fan was too important to be switched off at that moment. He reviewed the scenario of his meeting with the princess and her friend on that Sunday evening in the sitting room. He thought of it over and over again. Confused whispers now covered his lips. "Really beautiful" "Looked descent" It was too strange; a sudden jerk up in the middle of the night with such whisperings. He was submissive to his thoughts as though he was before God for a need. Who knows if that was the exact reason that made his being so silent and concentrative like a poor man pushing crates of eggs in a wrecked wheelbarrow on a crummy little street in the worst part of the town. He was summoned off by the long click sound of the minute hand of the wall clock and a smart movement of the hour hand after whirling, indicating a change in hour's time. He was totally carried away by his emotion. He no longer made it to sleep the night, till it dragged by.

VIII

The gentle sun rise and was radiant in a clear blue sky, the pinks and yellows of the sunrise glinted on the window glasses of a decorated self-contained building like the glint of a hot sun on water in a river, well roofed with green slate. The environment was cool and silent as though it had rained a day before with a pervaded scent of some beautiful flowers that surrounded the four walls of the building. The building was hired by Agwaza for Mdoo and Afa. Mdoo had just finished washing and tidying up the rooms. She was about to prepare the lunch. It was Saturday so they had no lecture, not even a fixed one from some lecturers, who liked to have fixed lectures on Saturdays. After being late in their onus, they would come late to bombard students with assignments, lots of tests as well as long lasting lectures that often lost almost half of the class before it ended and at times more than half of the class. Afa would not give a damn about it. What a relief this Saturday!, Afa felt surprised for such to happen at the tail end of the semester, when she had not heard of any death of a student, neither an urgent meeting by staff. So far so good she had no cause to feel guilty this Saturday, it was a special day for Afa to party with friends as usual. A day to leave early for party and come back in the early hours of the next day when the cock will be on its feet after dusting its self from muck and stretching its neck with its peak wide open in the air to crow, while the day adjusts its garment to light the dawn. She had smiled amusedly with her one leg crossed over the other in the parlour watching a program on a television set with much excitement written all over her face. "I have a day again; a special day to show my skills tonight. A day I will dance and wind my waist up and down in a zigzag style in front of men, a day to shake my hips rhythmically on the blasting sound of music and drag all men in a state of sheer lunacy" she murmured to herself and laughed again. "Yes… Yes" she whispered with her head nodded in agreement or rather content She seemed comfortable. "I got to put on the new white short tight jeans skirt, and my new show-belle and set-on-breast jacket over my white singlet and also the white trainers" she added with content. "Shout out to all the men, let them get lust. I got to rock the night," she shrieked again in amusement now it was little bit audible. Mdoo came out of the kitchen; she served Afa a full plate of delicious meal of rice, beans and plantain with a separate plate of stew. The aroma of the food alone was enough indication that it was tasty. It was indeed delicious. Afa ate the meal slowly, savoring every mouthful. She had neither simple compliment to give nor thanks for the meal. Eating was not a problem to her but only to concoct a little meal of any kind was like sending a goat to arrest a hyena in its kingdom which is obviously impossible for the goat to return back with a positive result if at all it had managed to survive. Now it mastered her. What could she bring out of the kitchen to serve? Was there anything? –Nothing, -just nothing, a woman at twenty two could offer not even warm water. Afa's carefree attitude and poor culinary skills benefited Mdoo greatly. What could she not do? She had always been up to her task. Mdoo would hardly forget her experience with Ngodoo whenever in the kitchen. If not a heavy knock on the head, it would be a plate on the head; if not pepper in the eyes, it would be hot water on her body. What had Ngodoo not done to Mdoo?. Using her artificially fixed nails to pierce Mdoo's skin was just a fair act for her, she would not mind. Blood would trickle across her body. Beatings and provocative utterance were rained on her on daily basis. But all these, never did she report to Agwaza. He was seldom at home, although he knew the kind of woman he had for a wife. Agwaza would sense something from Mdoo's mood many a times he comes back home. But even if he asked, she would say all was well. She would endure the ill-treatment with stoicism. Since the briefs of his work would not permit him to be home at anytime, his usual closing time became a special alarm for her to play eye service. He knew what his wife was capable of doing; pitying Mdoo in his presence wasn't genuine enough for him to be deceived easily. He could not remember when she started being generous. He trusted his wife very well to have been dangerous and decisive more than a chameleon. He had known all these but hence Mdoo would give no report, he had nothing to do. He had not forgotten how she disgraced him to his friend. She had instructed Tersoo; who was staying with them one day to frog-jump without foot wear in the sun after accusing him of stealing her money. The frog-jump lasted for long as if that wasn't enough. He asked him also to stand in the sun on the tips of his toes while his soles did not touch on the ground. His height reduced, and his knees bent forward and his hands spread forward like the posture of a cyclist on a motorcycle, coupled with beatings that he would hardly forget in his life time. She always made sure he ate little food in the house. Ngodoo usually beat Tersoo mercilessly and at the end she would blunt it with threats. "If you dare report to Agwaza and I get to know, just imagine yourself sitting on a hot stove, imagine yourself as a goat being a guest in hyena's house, imagine yourself in the pit of dens without an angel, and imagine yourself as a calabash in the clumsy fingers of drummers. I will make sure you starve to death." She had often said bitterly with wrath in her eyes. Tersoo would only cry, he would have nothing to do than to grin and bear it, he got used to it. If not, what could he have done then, when he had just spent only a few months and some few days in a place where he knew no one, not an aunt, not an uncle, neither a sister, nor brother of his had ever been. His father was in the village with his mother struggling with their predicaments after his father had dropped out of school in form five because he had no one to sponsor him. Since he had been brought there, Tersoo had only known his neighbors to be the thick tall painted walls of the fence that led to the giant and high quality gate of the house. So could he report to the walls or the gate? No way, he had to bear it. Like a war another day came. Agwaza went to work, Mdoo and Afa had also gone to school but Tersoo was at home waiting to start school by first term since it was a third term. Tersoo had finished the portion of work Ngodoo assigned to him. He had not eaten since morning and it was few minutes to one o'clock. He was weak, weak as though he was recovering from a troublesome ailment. His stomach ached, coupled with dizziness. Ngodoo had instructed him not to eat until she returns from where she went. He could no longer swallow his spit again. He stood from his seat feeling cold and scared. He matched to the kitchen, feeling weak and his hands were very heavy to turn the knob on the kitchen door. A bell rang deep down in his heart summoning his thoughts; his heart missed a beat and wobbled, and before it inert, one of his thoughts stroked in a question. "What did you think you are doing?" "To fetch food and eat of course" the other thoughts swiftly interfered. "Why would you do such a thing?" his thoughts gave in another question, the question was too heavy for him, he stood still like a wall in dilemma for some time and his thoughts again persisted. "You have to do it can't you see that you are hungry and tired? "You better not do it" the other now powerfully interjected "Go ahead and do what you want to do" "I tell you mummy would not let you go scot free" it warned again. His heart could not miss a beat now; he stood transfixed with shock in his attempt to prevent his over heart beat but to no avail and now it was beating more and more. He felt a swirl that growled in his stomach as his thoughts went on battling. And other one drew a note of finality. "You better go and eat, and stop starving yourself even though you eat the food or not, you can't still escape the beatings, how would she ever trust and free you? You better eat, get energy and prepare for what will come". And then he gave in, he turn the knob and entered the kitchen, he saw some plates piled up so he quickly picked one and fetched a little quantity of the food; he came out and sat in front of the house in between the two mighty poles that supported the building and provided shade also, facing the gate directly. He had taken up to six spoons of the food and with a drink of water to stretch his intestine when the gate opened. Without waste of time, a right leg first entered, followed by the left one and then the whole body. It was Ngodoo who had returned from her friend's house. Tersoo got insight of her, his hand dropped off the spoon of rice he had raised to his mouth and at the same time he was trembling. Ngodoo had seen him very clearly. "What!" she sneered "What did you think you are doing?" Tersoo jolted up at once, he could not answer the question, the same question his thoughts gave earlier and now came Ngodoo. She pounded on him by giving him severe beating and asked him to kneel on the covers of bottles from the side that grips the bottle's head under the sun with a mortal placed on his hands up in the sky. Unfortunately that day, while Tersoo was still on the punishment crying, the gate suddenly opened and-wham! – it was Tersoo's mother who had come to visit them. It was terrible Tersoo's mother could not keep to it and that was how she made away with her son in Agwaza's absence. Afa was still in the parlour murmuring and laughing as though she was out of her mind or the program she was on, was the belt of the amusement, so composed, submissive and concentrative to her thoughts. It was not a mistake to have bought the new party dresses. "No more mess in this next party, that was too unexposed no man would be patient enough to buy an apple in a black water proof and then take it home before getting sight of it" she had rebuke herself about her last party wears. "I must appear sexy to capture," she had now finalized. She had not forgotten what happened in the last party. How she was not given much attention when ladies that came to the party in a grand style were glittering more than glasses in the sun, in the eyes of men, looking flashy like diamond in the fluorescent lights of the club.

IX

As the day passed by, the sun reduced its fierce rays and everywhere became calm and cool. Afa was still in the sitting room while Mdoo was in the bedroom. She had just finished taking her bath and was dressing when a flashy ash coloured Peugeot 406 model stopped in front of their building. Two persons came out of the car, a man and a lady. Mdoo peeped through the window and saw it was her friend; Shimana and her brother Kamimi, she walked out and welcomed them into the sitting room. Mdoo was very happy for their visit. Afa also welcomed them happily. It was a thing of joy in their midst. "How are you doing?" the prince asked confidently after he sighed heavily from his seat. "We are fine" Mdoo and Afa answered at the same time. "I am happy to see you" Mdoo said with a wave of hand referring to the prince and her friend. "Happy to see you too" they reciprocated the excitement. It was a very beautiful moment for them. "I am surprise to see you in our apartment. I hope all is well?" Mdoo said smilingly referring to Kamimi. He glanced swiftly at all of them and the corners of his lips were now in the fountain of a smile; so lovingly. His mouth opened a little and a genuine masculine voice was heard as he spoke out. "No...No, come-on all is well; actually we are out today to visit special friends. We've just left my friend's house and here we are." "Wao, that's nice; that's to say am special then" Mdoo said and everyone laughed. "Yaa… you are, Mdoo" Kamimi said receiving backing words from Shimama. "Mdoo how is the weekend going?" Shimana asked Mdoo. "It's going smoothly, we bless God. I intended visiting you today but eventually decided for tomorrow and fortunately here you are" "Oh, that was a nice intention and what makes you think our visit has deterred your coming to see us, just take it that today is a different day and tomorrow comes another different day so I will be much more expecting you," they all laughed out loud. Afa was in their midst so quiet but from time to time she would laugh to their jokes and her presence was not forgotten. Mdoo stood-off quietly from their midst but on return she brought some meal for them. They were glad with her hospitality. Kamimi would from time to time release his masculine voice very gently and allow his lips extend a little backward as it creates some dimples on his cheeks. They discussed among themselves for some time. When Kamimi and Shimana wished to leave, Mdoo and Afa followed behind to see them off. Kamimi said to Mdoo with a smile, "I think we should have you visited as well, I have something to tell you". Mdoo quickly turned to Afa and to the princess she could see clearly without dizziness or cobwebs obstructing her view as her friend nodded her head like a lizard in agreement and then she turned back to the prince, her looks seemed she was up to say "What for? I would not be chanced" but surprisingly she sounded. "By God's grace I will your highness". Now it was enough for Afa, her thought has now been confirmed. Shimana and Kamimi got into their car. Mdoo and Afa bid them goodbye and watched as they got out of sight. All through their stay in the sitting room Afa felt tensed, she was disturbed by Kamimi's expression towards Mdoo and now the invitation. "There must be something" she had attested within herself. This was what she could not waste a minute before asking Mdoo. "Who are they?" Afa fussed out on their way back to the sitting room. "Don't you know my friend princess Shimana again?" "I know I mean the man with him" "He is her brother" "What is your relationship with him?" "What relationships are you talking about? He is the brother of my frie…" "But I heard him inviting you and saying he has something to tell you, what for?" she debatefully interrupted. "That I don't know" Mdoo said sincerely with her two hands spread before her chest gesticulating her words. "Serious…okay, fine" Afa said sarcastically and shrugged her shoulders. The princess and her brother's visit have played a drum of thinking to Afa and Mdoo. It was left for them now to choose a dancing style. Afa interpreted what happened differently, so did Mdoo. Afa's heart was now set on the Prince. She had barely recollected the scene that took place in the sitting room, the tablet of her heart was completely occupied with the Prince's image. The Prince's voice reincarnated, it rumbled heavily and whirled deep down in her heart, it echoed audibly, and she became vulnerable. A sudden cold engulfed her and set her emotionally unbalanced and instantly she desired him. But was she also attracted to him? Yes, that was the question. But that alone was not a challenge to Afa as she had worked out things for herself many times. Her worries were the Prince's expression toward Mdoo but not withstanding, for any madness Afa had proven to have a chain for its patient. Mdoo on the other hand was rather anxious of what the prince had to talk with her. She thought very much about it. Mdoo was a lady who was very anxious about things that would happen in the future. Many thoughts whirled in Afa's heart while she was back in the sitting room. As the time crossed half passed seven in the evening, her alarm sounded and she jerked up reluctantly as though she was forced by someone. She prepared herself for the intended party. She dressed exactly as she had planned. Mdoo saw her dressing. It was a-stand-still shock for Mdoo. What baffled her about ladies had now emerged under her roof. She could not believe herself seeing Afa dressed like professional prostitutes without fear. "Afa what kind of dressing is that?" Mdoo asked Afa out of care but she turned and gave Mdoo an egregious look full of hatred, a look that expressed anger and detest. "Not dressings for adopted children." She snide furiously and again snapped "Don't forget to leave the door open today oo…" she banged the door in rage and walked out of the house. It was painful. So painful that Mdoo moved from the sitting room to the bedroom like a dizzy old man, with tears rushing out from her eyes like water from a broken pipe. She wept bitterly as though she had received death news of a beloved one. Afa had slapped Mdoo's heart, with words that were only used by her mother and today came Afa. She cried till her eyes became red like the eyes of a smoker. It had now reached a stage that she would not keep silent. Agwaza must hear it this time around. As a matter of fact she was not going to leave it, she must come to the root of it. She would no more let Agwaza continue caging her in that mystery while her blood keeps on boiling with snide remarks of adopted child from Ngodoo and Afa. With bitterness in her heart she contended to report to Agwaza. So many thoughts whirled around her mind.

X

Mdoo moved with a man arms in arms into a garden plant with brightly coloured leaves and flowers, both of them were excited. They matched to a long white painted iron chair; the chair had been mounted in the garden so white like the clothes they were putting on. He sat on the chair, Mdoo laid slump and snuggled her head into his laps, her eyes straight into his, and then they whispered to each other and play with rose flowers in their hands. After a while he raised her up into the sky and turned her round and sing lullaby like the mother does to her child when petting the child to sleep or for milk. After that she was running and the man pursued her round and round of the begonia, she later ran and hid at one edge of the flowers in the garden but he saw her and ran over to her. He embraced her in his arms, closed his eyes and stretched forward to kiss her forehead and there and then the door slide open making a quin…quin… sound and some steps followed announcing human movements, just then Mdoo opened her eyes on the bed. Afa had returned from the club in the early hours of the day. It was the dawning of

Sunday as usual, she flung her hand bag on a chair in the sitting room and staggered onto the bedroom and flopped on the bed so exhaustive as though she had offloaded a truck load of cement. Mdoo stood up from her bed and prepared some water to take her bath and get ready for her morning services. She had not forgotten that she had to visit Kamimi later the day, moreover she was already anxious, so she could not forget to meet up with the appointment. She felt a sudden excitement while she was bathing she imagined what really brought the joy, but she could not figure out what it had been, but the excitement kept thrilling inside of her. Strange, too strange for one to all of a sudden feel happy without any reason, or was she becoming like a lizard that always nodes its head upon falling from a tree. The excitement had compelled her to think of its reasons. Would it have been her dreams or her appointment with the prince that she had no idea of? Or what was it then?

XI

The sun had lowered from where it had climbed so high up in the centre of the sky so that a man lost his shadow. The clouds whirled round and round, darkening the sky in the North east side of the country, that by the sign astronauts would explain to be symptoms of rainfall but this time it was not so and the skies were cleared. Mdoo had made it to the palace. She met Kamimi and her friend at home. They had been sitting under a shade in the house when she walked in. Kamimi was indeed grateful for her honouring the invitation. None of the minutes spent in their midst had gone without laughter. He was greatly known for that, whenever he meant to poke fun, none would have the courage to resist it. They had very exciting moments. She was at ease now. Speaking with him became less difficult for her because he was open. She found it comfortable and exciting. Not too long as they were discussing, Shimana excused herself leaving him with Mdoo. She seemed suspicious but he dimmed it off immediately he observed it. "You are looking so good in your outfit," he initiated the conversation complementally. "Really?" Mdoo gave in with smiles. "Sure, I like the dressing," he added. "Nice to know your wish is like mine" "I desire to know the one who sew for you" "Oh no… it sound funny, what for?" "So I could look like you" "But you are already looking good in these ones you put on, sorry I forgot to compliment at first, whereas my seamstress is a professional only in women dresses" "Oh there I miss," they all laughed. As soon as silence was restored, he leaned forward on his seat and looked straight into her eyes. "Mdoo," he called and continued "Certainly I needed your attention that was why I desired to see you. I want you to know how much I feel for you. I love you so much and I want you to be my wife." She quickly gazed her eyes on him as soon as she heard those words. She was surprised. Her heart jumped but she managed to speak. "I'm afraid my prince that won't be possible, don't tell me, you don't know my relationship with your sister" "I do. I know that she is your friend, but I love you so much can't you see it?" "Kamimi, Shimana is my best friend, and I can't do this to jeopardize our relationship. I am sorry I think I should be on my way," she said and stood up to leave. After she had left, he spoke with his sister about it and she promised to talk to her friend.

XII

Few weeks later Mdoo fell for Kamimi's advances. People would say love emerge by first sight, that was true for Mdoo and Kamimi. It happened the first day they saw each other in the sitting room of the palace. They had understood it well that something had transpired between them on their very first sight. They were drenched in a stream of love; it was left for the physical to decide after the minds had concluded speaking through the means of eyes contact. It was what Mdoo had never experienced before in her life. She had seen many young men looked at her in the eyes with admiration but that sharp look that day from Kamimi was unusual. It was very striking and very charming. It displayed her emotions, if not for her high sense of self-control she was already falling. She thought whether she was being stupid but on a second thought she dismissed that thought. The reversible reaction within their hearts worth beyond her thought of stupidity. But to keep it normal then, they both interpreted it meaningless. Kamimi testified one day when they were together, how he felt on the first day he met her and how he was only trying to be a gentle man in her sister's presence. Kamimi had become the first image on the page of Mdoo's heart. She loved him so much. They were compatible like pair of gloves. Mdoo had never dreamt of loving him that way. The love she had for him was indeed great. She could not even believe herself of a day in his house. How she gathered the courage to tell the prince right in the face that it will be impossible for them to be together, for the reason of his sister being her bosom friend even though she felt for him also. But she could not spit in her tea. She thought whether it was unwise for her to have said those words to the prince deterring his burning love for her in the name of her friendship with the princess. But on the contrary she had made an astute move, for he had confided to his sister how much he loved her and also pleaded with his sister to be with Mdoo. Shimana had approved, and had also given guidance, but she never called her friend to discuss it with her. Rather, she then placed her on a trial to know intimately the kind of friend she really was, and fortunately she had it right. She was very surprised when her brother told her that Mdoo disapproved for the reason of their friendship, it was shocking to her, just as it was when she wanted to convince her on behalf of her brother. Not only had she been wise but she had also placed an image of integrity on herself. She was complete without blemish in the eyes of Kamimi and Shimana. He loved Mdoo so much that their love could take hours to define. Unharmonious like kerosene and water was approximately the description of the relationship Afa planned to have with Mdoo, since she came to know that Kamimi had fallen in love with her. A man she so desired had now become the heart beat of Mdoo. She felt bitter. This was what would send someone six feet down, but who to go was the question. And to let go of Kamimi was what Afa would never think of. She had now planned to work things for herself, doing anything possible to retrieve him was the only thing she was now set for. Many efforts she made to charm and trap the prince had proved abortive. Her continued solitary mood with Mdoo seemed she had another plan.

XIII

So far so good, Mdoo had now graduated. She was very happy, she could not believe herself that she was now a graduate. She remembered when she was entering the campus gate and some students shouting at her "Year one" and some shouting "Jambito" but it eventually came to an end. It was what she thought was impossible. She could now close her eyes and remember the six years she was afraid of, it had now passed like six months. Agwaza was very happy to see Mdoo coming back home now as a graduate. It was shocking for him to imagine how time can fly. He now sighted her from the eyes of the heart, how she was small growing into a teenager and now a full grown lady. He saw how he used to carry her to school and now a Medical Doctor standing before him. Ngodoo had not yet denounced her hatred for Mdoo. She now felt sulkier about her. This was getting more serious. So serious to a point that she could no longer answer her greetings or talk to her any more. Her being a graduate was to Ngodoo like she had arrived, like she had achieved all in life. It gripped her so much that all the elements of hatred she had began to fuss out on Mdoo. Afa was very angry one Sunday afternoon when she heard Mdoo's conversation with the prince on a cell phone about his coming for marriage introduction. She felt like dying than to see it happen. She finally told her mother about it. Before the day would dawn it was too long for Ngodoo. She set her mind on many thoughts that whirled inside her throughout the night. As soon as it was dawn she took her bath and dressed with her daughter. They both entered into the street, very well prepared to answer any one that might ask where they were heading to. "To the market," would simply be their firm reply, "To get some food stuff" if at all any one asking needed more explanation about what they were going to do. But Agwaza was not even around, so who was there to ask, would Mdoo even dare to ask? How possible was it? If her greetings were rejected talk more of asking such a passionate question which needed an answer. Ngohile, Ngodoo's niece was a fair tiny smart little girl at the age of nine. She talked very much a parrot, not minding her structure and age. She loved Mdoo so much starting from the very day Mdoo came back from school. She rushed into her room after confirming properly the exit of Afa and her mother. As soon as she walked into her room, Mdoo sensed that Afa and her mother were not around. Ngohile's coming close to Mdoo was only possible in their absence, Ngodoo warned her of being close to her. The orders were only obeyed when Afa and her mother were around. She jumped on Mdoo's bed shouting "Aunty…Aunty" she was always happy whenever she was with her unlike Afa who found fault in whatever she did and always end up flogging her. "Aunty, have you eaten?" Mdoo was amazed by her question, she smiled and replied. "Yes I have eaten" "Aunty why is it that you are always inside your room when ever daddy is not around?" "It is nothing, I just feel like" Mdoo replied very quicky. "Why is it that when I want to come inside your room mummy and Afa would not let me?" The little Ngohile asked again. "Maybe they don't want you to be disturbing all the time" replied Mdoo. "Aunty, could you please stay with me in the sitting room so that I can watch television?" Ngohile requested politely. "I don't want to go to the sitting room, I am okay here," Mdoo expressed her satisfaction. "But aunty I want to stay with you" she insisted and Mdoo moved with her to the sitting room so she could watch television. Into the streets Afa and her mother stopped a taxi. "Where are you going to?" the taxi driver inquired. "This direction," Ngodoo said pointing her index finger straight upward. And the taxi driver followed. "Please be fast," Ngodoo demanded but rather unfriendly. The taxi driver complied swiftly. After 30 minutes thereabout the taxi descended a very high hill, before finishing with the slope another high hill awaited him to climb. Beside, was a very thick forest. As soon as the taxi driver climbed the second hill, Ngodoo ordered the taxi driver to alight. The taxi driver stopped and they rushed out. The taxi driver collected his money laughed and shook his head, Afa and her mother did not miss the action. Before they would ask him the reason for that he set off. Beside the road on the high hill, there was a dirty and unclear walk way that led into the dense forest like the walk way of cattle or a farm walk way of the old, very narrow that by morning during the rainy season, the dews would drench passersby. Ngodoo grab her daughter's left hand and entered the walk way into the forest. The forest was very dense, it had many tall trees like Prosopis africana, Khaya senegalensis, Parkia biglobosa, Vitellaria paradoxa, Daniellia olivera, Irvingia gabonensis and many others. Afa was afraid. She proposed to come back, but her mother insisted. Shortly, she sighted a glow of light in their front and the birds set on making terrible sounds, just then they entered a shrine. Ngodoo was not afraid, it seemed as if she had being visiting the shrine. She was very confident in her movement and actions. As soon as they approached the entrance of the province, she asked her daughter to remove her foot wear and enter backward till they finally entered the inner circle. Immediately they all turned, two mighty snakes that were on the shrine's throne embraced themselves and then changed into a giant old woman. She was so fearful to look at, so terrible, and immediately everywhere became dark, she dressed in black, her hairs were like an old village woman's afro and her teeth were very reddish like a fully ripped kola nut seller's own. She stared at both Afa and her mother and then gave a long laugh. "Ha… ha…ha…"she then pause and stood up and when she spoke there would be a long lasting echos. "My children… my children…" she sounded, "I know what brought you here, you…" she said and then pointed at Afa's mother and continued. "You want Mdoo's mind to be changed so that she will refuse to marry the prince and the prince in turn will marry your daughter and thereafter Mdoo would become mad." Again she stormed into her long lasting laughter. "Ha… ha… ha… ha…" "Is that not what you want?" The woman asked them. "Yes… yes…" they all chorused affirmatively. "Ha… ha… ha… ha…" she laughed again "That is a little offer I do for my children, just consider it done… just consider it don… ha… ha… ha…". Very terrible! Did she mean it? Was she really going to change Mdoo's mind? And turn her mad? How would it be? Mdoo was still with Ngohile in the sitting room she never imagined that in the next few minutes she would change her mind on the prince and become mad carrying dirty rags all round the market square with bunch of worthless items. She would dust and pile them, and begging for food and chasing little children with a whip. People would be astonished. They would stare at her, and point fingers and would say, "there she comes, the mad graduate." She would dress in rags, tie bottles and plates round her body, a black waste bin would be her food store. Kamimi under a spell would pass with Afa in a car and horn her to make way for them to pass. She would become a medical doctor on refuse dumps with many patients of her kind. The old woman was now set to make all these happen, she carefully positioned a wide calabash filled with water in her front and then she proceeded with reciting incantations. She bent before the calabash and called Mdoo's name three times seeking her face from the calabash so that she would strike. But nothing showed up, she then stood and walked backward to a living lion and shouted "pantheria leo tin tin..., pantheria leo gon gon..., pantheria leo don don...." The lion opened its mouth very wide she dip her hand straight inside and brought out a black small gourd. She danced side by side round the calabash with the gourd making some incantations "Ka nyi I lu shin kucha shin kucha kuruku a te kyav ve kpan a dugh ye mkuma ga..., Ngojov ôlun mese ... Torjov ôlun mese mdura ooo..." And then she opened the gourd and poured inside the calabash a yellowish gelatinous substance. Again she called Mdoo's name twice and as she called for the third time flame came out powerfully disappearing in the air and the calabash broke into pieces. There was no more darkness in the shrine. She smelled trouble. Afa and her mother also sensed that something had gone wrong. She now told them to go and come back in two weeks time that her gods were asleep. She held her daughter and they left the shrine. Ngodoo was very angry and upset that her wishes were not granted. All she wanted was to come back home and see Mdoo talking unlawfully about the prince to their hearing and give a lunatic laugh to show them that an intensive madness awaited her, and possibly by now folding some of her hair ties and shoes to her new destination. And the market square to meet her lunatic friends, by now putting her documents that had been torn into pieces in her small purse and calling it money so as to make her leave complete. But now she was coming back home to wait after two consecutive weeks before she would see someone she knew designs a shade on a refuse dump in the market square. This was too long for Ngodoo. Could she accept to wait for the two weeks? "Two weeks? That is too long I cannot wait," unanticipated she had said two days after she came back from the shrine. Ngodoo had capitalized she was going to do something about it, throw Mdoo in a pit of misfortune, very sure she was going to do it, and she was a woman of her words. She again made her way with her daughter to another shrine. But the same thing happened. This time it was the magician's mirror that broke into pieces immediately he called Mdoo's name. Ngodoo felt disappointed and without ado she started consulting her friends who later took her to another soothsayer in the locality, who could do and undo, who had done unimaginable things. So, they found their way to him too. But he told them that all the soothsayers and magicians were on a wrong track, narrating that any soothsayer who wants to view and charm Mdoo in any medium, would get his or her viewing medium broken, unless her three middle hairs were plucked and taken to the shrine. Since that was the only thing to make their plans work out, they were bent on getting even more than what the great magician had requested. In as much as it was a difficult task, a very difficult one, Ngodoo was ever ready to do anything possible for Mdoo to swim in misfortune and her daughter live happily. Even if it was for her to go without food for days and sleep naked for seven market night in the market square just for her daughter's comfort she was ready to do, than just to remove three middle hairs of a hag in less than 24 hours? She could possibly beat, force her with Afa and pluck away much more than just three hairs. "There is no problem with that I can do it even before 4 hours, set up the trap" Ngodoo had assured the magician earlier on. she was coming home with high tension, never minding whether Agwaza would be at home or not to make way with the element of her daughter's joy. Was Mdoo going to escape this? Had she known Afa and Ngodoo's plans on her? If at all she would have run then. Well, she was now equal with a blind man who could not identify a dirty clothe that is filled with perfume among neat ones, if one had not told him. When they arrived home, Mdoo had taken a trip to her friend's house.

XIV

Agwaza and his family all welcomed Kamimi and his sister with some of the royal council who had accompanied them for marriage introduction. This was another happy day for Mdoo and Agwaza too. The most important man of the day was smiles. He was seen on the faces of them that deserved him and joy speaking on the tablet of their hearts. Was this so with Afa and her mother? Were they as well going to smile? Smile with bitter kola in their mouth? How mysterious was this going to be. The heart had felt but could not explain to the eyes to produce tears, the eyes themselves had seen and were eager to produce tears, but the heart had neglected to give a message, rather the heart involved itself in conversation with the brain and both married to ache, delivering heartache and headache in the kingdom of pain. Afa and her mother refused to let their visitors see and understand their feelings rather they allow eyes service to play its drum. They prepared a delicious meal for the people and they all ate before enquiring about their mission to their house as the Tiv culture required. An old man very short with grey hairs, who seemed to be the oldest among all the king's men stood up and greeted Agwaza and his family and again released a well-to-do compliment to the power house. They all laughed to the wisdom of the old man in his gratitude and compliment. The echo had reached the ears of the birds and they took it high in the sky happily. As soon as silence was restored in their midst, Agwaza once again welcomed them all and then he offered a question to the oldest man. "Wantereme! What brought you and your people to my house?" the old man gently said; "Not of bad at all, it is of good to know why we are here. Yes it is true our people will say an eagle does not appear in the market without a reason, just as there is no smoke without fire. Our son's rib has been stolen and we are aware that the suspect is in your house which is the genuine reason of our coming" "It is very good of you to know where the suspect of your son's rib is, but I have two in my house which one owes your son's rib?" Agwaza said and the old man turned to the prince and then back to Agwaza and said "Mdoo is her name" Agwaza called out Mdoo from the house. "Do you know these people?" "Yes I do daddy" she replied. "Okay tell us who they are to you" Mdoo remained silent for some seconds and then replied. "The man here" she said pointing at the prince "Is my fiancé, the one that wants to marry me". Agwaza then permitted their wish. They were all happy to receive permission from Agwaza. They all expressed their gratitude to Agwaza and the family and assured the family to send a date for traditional marriage. It was much more than death experience to Afa and her mother. Ngodoo had never experience such a moment before, she felt much bitter, pains grip her flowing like blood all over her veins. The worst she had never expected had happened. All throughout the night she never let her eyes blink. She set her mind on other plans, if none would work, she was determined to eliminate Mdoo final. "It is better I eliminate her and face any consequences or die than to let this happen," she bitterly swore to herself that night. The next day evening the story seemed to have changed. Ngodoo felt happy with her daughter they laughed on and on in Afa's bedroom, what was it now? had they gotten another plan? Had they succeeded? Had they conquered? It seemed so. It seemed they had finished Mdoo. "Waoh what a mighty plan mummy, you stroke the bridge on the main pillar," Afa complimented her mother. They had arrived, yes indeed they had arrived. Nothing again was to be done; it was clearly seen on their faces. Afa and her mother laughed and laughed all day long. Mdoo had finished taking her bath she rushed into her bedroom to pick her call, but the call ended as she picked up the phone, it had appear to be the fourth missed call, it was the prince calling. She had no airtime in her cell phone to call back. She quickly dressed up so she could get airtime in a phone booth outside the house, and then the phone rang again by now it was not the prince but Shimana who called. "Hello dear!" Mdoo answered. "Hi, how are you?" "I am fine, and how about you?" "I am fine too, are you at home?" "Yes I am" "What's wrong? Prince told me you are not picking his calls" "Yeah, there is nothing wrong, I was in the bathroom when he called, he called about four times before I came out from the bath room and unfortunately the call ended and I had no airtime on my phone and I was about going outside to get before you called" "Yes that's what he told me, that he called four times but you did not answer, so don't worry I will tell him to call back now okay" "Alright thank you I appreciate bye" "Bye too" Without waste of time, prince called back. "Hello dear!" "Hi" "I called but you did not pick" "I'm sorry I was in the bath room when you called" "How are you doing?" "I'm fine, and you?" "Not fine at all" "What's wrong?" "Daddy had told me something and I'm very upset, I wish to see you so that we could talk about it" "What is it? Is it not what you will tell me on the phone?" "No, I need to see you, please meet me at Symbols Bar" "All right I will" "Thank you."

XV

Later in the day Mdoo came back so furious she stormed her room and then started wailing, she cried out loud. What was it now? What had made Mdoo wail and cried so loud? Had she lost any of her friends? What was it then? Why would she be screaming? Agwaza was at home he rushed from his room to see what had happen to Mdoo that she was screaming. On reaching there he saw Mdoo rolling on the ground with tears, Agwaza was sobbed. "What is it? Mdoo what is it? What is wrong with you?" he quickly asked. "Daddy why? Why? Daddy…" "What happen? Please tell me, what is it?" "Daddy what have I done? What have I done in this world to deserve this? God have you forsaken me?" Agwaza was confused. "Please my daughter stop crying, wipe your tears and tell me what the matter is" "Daddy what am I still doing on earth? Why am I living? Mummy reported to the king that I am an adopted child" "God of my ancestors" Agwaza wailed. He was shocked to hear it. He began to perspire, bobbles of sweat suddenly gathered on his brow, he was more confused and embittered. "Daddy the king said that the prince will not marry me, so why am I living? I want to die, I can't do without prince." Tears rushed out from one of Agwaza's eyes and rapidly descended down to his chin. He was totally confused. What was he going to do, was the only question that kept coming in his mind. He raised Mdoo up. "Stop crying." "Why would I stop crying? Daddy show me my parents; Show me where you adopted me, I am tired of this anguish; I have received enough from mummy. What has she not done to me? Show me where you adopted me. I can't do without prince". Agwaza was greatly annoyed, he put down his head. Mdoo began to cry again. He raised his head up and now it was his two eyes that were pumping out tears. This was now too heavy for him to keep to himself and then he began. "My daughter you are not an adopted child. It is now 22 years; your mother rented a room in one of our neighboring houses. She told us her husband, your father had driven her away, so she could not bear the shame of going back to her house. She then decided to rent a room on her own. She was a clothe dealer, by name Kpengadoo. She came to our house one evening and asked for a favor that she would leave you with us and travel to buy clothes and said she was going to stay for two days. I accepted and that was all about your mother. Since that day, no one has ever seen her. I traced her but to no avail, I had nothing to do then than to take care of you. You were very small about two years. By then I had no child. I had married Afa's mother and for over ten years, she was yet to conceive and I then married another wife, her name was Anapine, who was eight months pregnant she went to the market when I was not at home and she did not return. No one had seen her and I have had issues with her parents till today. My daughter if I knew where your mother is I would have taken you to her by now. I felt telling you before now would affect your life greatly. That was why I kept everything hidden. It was only I and my wife who knew about it" Mdoo felt a bitter disappointment and a sense of complete frustration. The entire house was pervaded by her perturbation.

XVI

Two days later the king summoned Agwaza and his entire family to his palace. What was it now? Has it come to the stage the king will have to summon Agwaza and his entire family? What was the summons for? What was the king now up to? Was it still about the issue of Mdoo an adopted child? Was the king now planning to do something extraordinary? Agwaza and his family honored the summons. It was still holiday, so Ngohile was the only one left at home. Mdoo was furious. So upset as she was going to sit and hear the king declare what he had against her love with the prince; and could she afford to really sit and listen to it? She stared around the palace's sitting room the environment that was going to witness her final agony or perhaps her death, for she had it that she could not do without the prince. The king's men were also in the palace sitting room. Kamimi and his sister were there with their step mother. Shortly after everyone had settled down, the king emerged from his room. Everyone stood still. They all greeted him at once "Zaa…ki" as he matched to his seat. "Mhmm… Msugh ne cii," he responded and further greeted everyone on seat. The king himself seemed upset, annoyance was already written on his face, he then said to Agwaza. "I have all of you summoned because dances are not going according to the beatings of the drum, and I want no more confusion. I am very disappointed. I asked my spokesmen to accompany the prince and my son for marriage introduction, of which they did and you all whole heartedly accepted. Two days back one of my spokes men reported to me that your wife seated here told him that Mdoo is an adopted child, and you know very well what that means…it is a taboo for me and my family to marry someone that has no identity. So I want to know, is it your wife that is saying the truth or you that permitted it to be. Let me hear and know your version. "Mdoo is not an adopted child," said Agwaza. "Is she your daughter then? For your wife had already refused that she is not her daughter." "Your highness, she is not my daughter." "But why then did you say she is not adopted if she is not your daughter? Why would you want to tarnish the image of my throne? The daughter that is not yours you accepted to be married to my son, the only prince of Mbaterem kingdom? Why should you act like this to me? "I am sorry your highness, but there was nothing I could do. Truly, Mdoo is not my biological daughter neither did I adopt her, so I had nothing to prove that I adopted her and if I had said she is adopted so the prince should not marry her and in turn she asked me to take her where I adopted her, what would I do your highness? For God knows that I did not adopt her, I can't decide negative on her. It is not my fault your highness. It is fate" "So how come about her, I mean who is she?" "Your highness it has been twenty two years now when Mdoo's mother by name Kpengadoo, a cloth dealer brought Mdoo to me. I was with my wife at home. It was on a Sunday evening. It was not long when she rented one room from our neighboring house, she wanted to travel to buy clothes and she came to us pleading if she could leave Mdoo with us and travel for the journey and I accepted. She told us she will come back in two days' time. She left and never returned. I traced for her but to no avail, and I decided to let Mdoo stay with me. That is why I cannot tell someone that she was adopted your highness" "But your wife said she was adopted by you," the king said, now in a pathetic voice. "Agwaza" he continued, "This is very pathetic, although she was not adopted but yet, she is of no identity. There is no much difference. There is a saying by our people that, an old lunatic does not throw stones but only gathers. But these stones can't be gathered. I cannot play tricks with the gods, I promise not to say this again." The king now sounded on a note of finality. Mdoo jumped up in agony, she flopped to the ground and started rolling in tears. The worst had happened. The road has come to an end. There is no two ways about it. Death was the next thing Mdoo was waiting for. "I cannot live without prince," she had often said. She turned and looked at the prince, two great drops of tears waded down his cheeks and he bent his head. As the king stood to dismiss everyone and then leave, an aged woman of about fifty years or so, stormed inside the palace parlour. She was averagely tall, chocolate in complexion, she tied a traditional scarf of black and white colours and another one slung on her shoulder. She was pleased to stare at. As she approached their midst, Agwaza dabbed his eyes to clearly see. Ngodoo was as well stretching her eyes to see clearly who had shown forth. The face seemed familiar to Agwaza and his wife. There was no doubt by their expression, or were they seeing an apparition? At once they both shouted "Kpengadoo!" "Yes it is me," the woman said nodding her head in agreement. "Jesus Christ!" Agwaza expressed his shock. "Yes is me Kpengadoo" "No…No…No…, this must be an apparition, I can't believe this" Ngodoo trembled. "No… No… I am not a ghost, this is real me, fill me, I am alive" Agwaza was shocked, Ngodoo was already shivering. "Your highness," Agwaza now called on to the king. He seemed to have got a solution to a sleep away-with kind of mathematics question solved without doubt. Happiness began to emerge. "Your highness, this is Kpengadoo, the woman I said gave Mdoo to me. Mdoo's mother, the clothe dealer." The king was still standing and then he turned to Mdoo. "Mdoo, this is your mother." Mdoo was shocked but happy. She ran and embraced her mother. It was like a fictitious movie, consciously planned and like a set up perpetually arranged to fit in. But never was it so. At times to believe what nature covers seems difficult to people. The king was surprised. Kamimi and the princess felt relieved. Joy began to save inside of them as sadness suddenly packed out. The king's men were perplexed. They stared at the woman with their eyes full of hatred as a mother who dumped her child. Afa and her mother were terrified. They became dumfounded. They were only staring with their mouth widely open. The king sat back and watched them incredulously. Kpengadoo moved with Mdoo in her arms to a seat. The warm hands of joy engulfed Mdoo gently. "Yes, I have found my mother." Mdoo said jubilantly under her breathe. "How come did you find yourself here in the king's palace?" Agwaza asked Kpengadoo. "This is about two weeks now that I have being having nightmares throughout about

Mdoo. I had the same nightmare for more than six times so I decided to come and check for her. For my conscience could not let me. When I came, I went to your house, but you people were not around. I only saw a little girl and she told me you were summoned by the king. I was confused so I decided to come to the palace." "Okay" Agwaza nodded his head. Ngodoo had clearly heard what Kpengadoo said. That Ngohile directed her. Ngohile was going to die today, how could she be the one to butter Mdoo's bread, when she needed sand to top Mdoo's little bread? Ngohile is today going to answer her ancestors from the grave; giving vivid answers to strangers will be no more. If one had two lives, Ngohile was going to die double, for she had bitten more than she could chew. Ngodoo was very, very sad. She and her daughter were very sad. Kpengadoo's arrival was a sting of a scorpion on a wet body to them. Kpengadoo made some steps toward Agwaza and she knelt before him and then she started tendering apologies with her cheeks covered with tears. "Agwaza I am very sorry, I am very very sorry for what I did to you. I lied to you that I was going to come back after two days and it was not so. Please I am so sorry, forgive me, please forgive me" Agwaza lifted her up to her feet "Stop crying I forgive you, stop crying kpengadoo, it is okay," he said and patted her shoulder. "What you came and met here was a terrible scenario. It was only your presence that held everything that was fast going to happen. The prince here is in love with your daughter, he wants to marry her and the tradition has it that a royal one cannot marry someone of no identity, and since you told me nothing about her, I had no single information about her and that means they won't solemnize the marriage. The king was placing his last words when you came in. It is God that wants it this way, we are very happy to see you, so wipe away your tears and talk to his highness as mother in-law so that he will find his way to your husband's house and your daughter will be married to her love" Kpengadoo began to weep again. Now she was shaking her head while crying. "What is it again, I said I have forgiven you," Agwaza said wondering her continued weeping. "No… Agwaza, I am afraid Mdoo is not my biological daughter" "Immediately as kpengadoo announced her not being Mdoo's biological mother, tears flew down Mdoo's cheeks. She began to cry loud and lamented for the flared up of her misfortune. "What a wicked world is this? What am I destined to be? What have I done to deserve this kind of mysterious life? What kind of a miserable life am I living? Life without parents, life without a home like bush animals," she cried and cried. It was so terrible she wept helplessly like a blind one thrown in the middle of the river. Afa and her mother had the moment as their happiest moment. Since pretence could not prevail against reality it became obvious. Agwaza was shocked to hear that from Kpengadoo. "Kpengadoo is Mdoo not your biological daughter?" questioningly he reiterated "Yes she is not my own daughter" "But you told us that she is your daughter when you came new in our neighboring house?" As soon as she said, her face showed sign of regret why she had spoken those words. "What will become of my little damsel, will this really prevent her from marrying the one she loves? Would she ever find anyone like the prince again? Or will she be lonely and then continue this miserable life with a broken heart? This is too much for a young girl like this, she had really suffered… But I don't think I will do her good if I deceive the king's family and the family of Agwaza and in the sight of God almighty. And then bring curse to myself, to her and the king's family. Let me give nature its own way," Kpengadoo had intensively thought and bowed down her head. Everyone was astonished. "Then whose daughter is she?" Agwaza asked. She sighed deeply and then raised her head up. Now a state of tranquility was prevailing in their midst, except the long sighing of Mdoo. They were all eager to hear her response.

XVII

"In my lonely days after I had been pursued by my

husband for not giving him a child after our six years of marriage. He refused to stay with me again. I can remember he had often said, he would not continue to stay with a man pretending he had a wife. I was forcefully thrown out of the house like a mad dog. I felt ashamed to return back to my people, I then decide to rent a room in the town to stay, where I later relocated beside your house. One night when I was in my room, the rain was pounding down on the thin roof and thunder rumbling in distance. I heard a thump on my door. When I opened the door it was my step brother. He was with a pregnant woman, they were all drained. I asked him why he came to my place in the middle of the night with a woman and who she was. He told me he knew nothing about her that he was sent to kill her but when he saw her pregnant, his conscience could not let him. So he decided to spare her. He told me that he negotiated with her that if she would not announce him he will free her. According to my brother he made her swore for her life. He asked me to take care of her and that after she has given birth, I should let her go. He charged me not to tell anyone that if by mistake anyone hears of it he will be killed. I cried in my heart, if at all my brother had listened to me he would not have involved himself in such kind of things. I got bitter at the same rate my heart was thumping. I hated to be called a sister to that kind of human being. I wished our father was alive so I could report it to him. Though our mothers were alive but they were all children in their minds. He was the only son of our father among the three wives our father had. Though I was scared, but I loved him so much, there was nothing I could do. I quickly took her inside my room and then he ran away and ran out of the town. That was how Mdoo's mother came to be with me. I wanted to ask her about herself when we were together but I was scared for my brother had warned me never to seek for any information about her nor tell her about myself for what so ever reason. Anytime she wants to tell me anything about herself as a woman to woman, I would change the conversation to another thing else or excuse myself from her with a reason. She was a very nice woman. After three weeks, I was outside washing her clothes while she was in the room. I heard her screaming so when I rushed in, I discovered her delivery period was almost. I quickly took her to the hospital, and after an hour she successfully delivered a bouncing baby girl. But the doctor refused that she should not be discharged, that she was not strong enough. Two days after, I did not understand her anymore as she was not getting better every hour. Even though as it was, I kept believing that nothing would happen. This time around the temptation that engulfed me was great, I had thought if anything happens to her what would I do? It is better for me to ask her so that if anything happen I would report to her people. Though I was not praying for anything to happen but I was apprehensive. And instantly it dawned on me, I remembered the implications. My heart stirred the more, what could I do again? I managed and resisted the urge. The next day when the baby was sleeping I went to buy pap and when I was coming back I heard her calling my name, our ward was down stairs, I ran in. She asked me to give her the baby, I told her the baby was sleeping but she insisted that I should bring her the baby, she held her and then smiled. But I was confused when I saw tears dropping from her eyes. Well, maybe that was just tears of joy, I thought so. She kissed her forehead and then stared at her again. She gave her back to me and said. "Her name is Mdoo, please take care of her. God will bless you for what you have done Please keep her safe." My heart got thumped for those words "please keep her safe," even as I said I will and told her that nothing would happen, yet those words were still strange to me. They were ringing inside of my head. Now it was no more what I thought earlier, she asked me to come close to her, she held my hand tightly, she coughed and sighed deeply, that was her end. I felt cold, but it was not the right time for me to play childishly. I then took Mdoo and sneaked out of the hospital, and when I came back I decided to pack out to where I was staying beside you." "Jesus" Mdoo shrieked and screamed, she dashed herself to the floor. Agwaza suddenly looked fierce. His mouth was left opened if not for his facial expression the flies could have made a home there in. The tragedy of the story stormed in with pains and over whelmed them. They were never expecting such. After all they waited for patiently was just a junk in the trunk. Mdoo had seen how her misfortune was moving from probative to infinitive level. The king watched Mdoo rolled in tears. He felt pity how her situation was rapidly elevating in misfortune. If not for the values of the tradition, the king was ever now ready to decide the best for her. "What on earth had the parents of this little lady done for her to reap this way? She had really suffered," the king had said in his mind. The atmosphere was tensed, nothing could have prevented the fierce heat that set in. It was terrible. "Did you mean she died without telling you anything about herself?" the king asked Kpengadoo. "Yes your highness if she had called the name of her husband while telling me Mdoo's name, I would have found it easy tracing her father, and to me I never thought death was embracing her. I would have voiced out" "So that means we cannot get Mdoo's parents?" Agwaza asked but Kpengadoo could not answer back, she sighed heavily and bowed down her head. "What about your step brother?" Agwaza asked Kpengadoo with anxiety in his eyes. "Yesterday when I came, I went to his house to my utmost surprise, he is a changed man, an evangelist. He told me that all started when he came back from 16 years imprisonment. That he searched for me all over but he could not find me. I told him what had happen to the woman she left with me to take care of, I told him how I left Mdoo with my neighbor and got married. I told him about my severe nightmares about Mdoo in my husband's house and how I come to find out about her. He was shocked. He said he will come with me and plead with you and also see how she is, but when we were about to come, his pastor came and they were discussing. He told me that I should show him the way he will meet me shortly. "When I was coming I took some of my photographs that I snapped with Mdoo's mother." She took her hand bag, brought out some photographs and gave them to Agwaza. "Yes this is the woman," she said pointing at the woman in the picture Agwaza collected the photograph. He jerked up all of a sudden and shrieked loud "Jesus! Oh my goodness," he shivered and the photograph fell on the floor. Mdoo rushed towards him. "What is it?" the king asked Agwaza with surprise. "Your highness my wife… she is my wife… my second wife Anapine." "You mean your wife?" "Yes your highness" "Look at it your highness," he said and collected the photograph from Mdoo and gave it to the king. Ngodoo was shocked to see Anapine with Kpengadoo in the photograph. Kpengadoo was baffled. What fate! Agwaza turned to Mdoo. "Mdoo I am your biological father, come…come… my daughter." He embraced her and tears went on dancing on their cheeks. It was like a dream, joy fell on Mdoo like the dew fall. She was invigorated for knowing that she was not a child of no identity but Agwaza's biological daughter, which verily signified the broken resistance of her marriage proceedings. Just then a man came in, it was Kpengadoo's step brother Kator. Ngodoo's heart got thumped immediately she set her eyes on him "What! Bunde oo, shabu tereme!" she exclaimed. "Kator are you alive?" "Yes I am alive" "Oh Kator you know this people?" Kpengadoo asked her brother. "No, I know only this woman. She was the one who gave me the deal to kill that woman I left you with." Everyone was astonished. Ngodoo fell down and went into a comma for days and never recovered consciousness. Few days after the trap for Mdoo failed Afa left home insane, celebrating with lunatics on dust bins...

VIRTUE OF SILENCE

I

My name is Tako Keghnen but my friends call me T.K for short. It was just after I had graduated as a medical doctor from the prestigious university of Nigeria Nsukka, Enugu State. After the dribs and drabs style of learning full of pains and stress that I married Iveren, my loving wife, very lively, beautiful and charming. She was dark in complexion, indeed an epitome of black beauty, perhaps it was from her that the great Nigerian musician 2face got the inspiration of the song he sang "…You are my African queen..." not only that it puzzled me still and I often thought if Flavour had seen her before he sang "…Ada ada…" She was actually a Jos tomato. Her body was smooth like that of an infant. She was tall, she had a pointed nose, her eyes were completely white, and her structure was excellently formed. When she speaks one feels dreamy and to birds they suddenly gets ignited with excitement on hearing her voice, and without perching, they make melodies and swiftly fly to inform the sun so to distribute its rays to the planets. Indeed her creator had diligently and carefully done a great job without an iota of error. She was very pleased to look at. No one would stare at her and hesitate for a minute to give another glance. Whenever depressed people looked at her they go back with testimonies of liberty. The most striking thing in her was her smiles. It formed out dimples that would render one uncomfortable. Whenever she smiled one would feel they had seen a star in the day time, how odd it might look but was the suitable description. That was how peculiar she seemed in the midst of many women around. I had not seen the most beautiful woman in the whole world but my wife was to be reckoned as the second most beautiful woman in the whole world if at all there was any to be the first. People would say beauty lies in the eyes of the beholder but this cliché never seems to work on her, her beauty was obviously reflective to all that sighted her. We first met way back in secondary school at Government Day Secondary School, Buter. It was on a Monday morning. There was no teacher in our class. Although it was not a free period but the teacher on duty had given a correspondence that he was traveling, so I decided to pick the subject of the period and read. Some of my mates were also reading while some were chatting among each other. I would from time to time chuckle to myself as I read my note book. I chuckled again later on as I reflected on how my teacher would teach us the subject and demonstrate, beguiling us with tales in a sense of humor. We would laugh and comprehend Economics very well. Everyone loved Economics because of Sir Stingers. No one sleeps in his class even a pregnant woman cannot afford it. He was indeed a genius. If at all the whole world has me to show a very good tutor in Economics, there would be no wasting of time in commending him, but today he was not around we all missed him. As I smiled quietly this time, I leaned back at the immediate desk of my mate with my eyes closed unto the ceiling and shortly I heard some footsteps in that I presumed to have been a teacher. Who had been so workaholic to take the chance of another teacher? I questioned myself inwardly and my eyes opened at a snail's pace. I was flabbergasted and my heart could not escape a beat. It gave a hard thump that made me felt it had gone out of its asylum and was about to descend down to diaphragm. But I got attested when it repeated rapidly and audibly that one close could hear, all as a result of a lady that came in with my classmate, Dooshima. My desk was second in the middle row. She had clearly sighted me and had seen how I reacted. I had no single way to deny the fact and I could sense it that she knew very well what had happened. My eyes could not stand the sharp lightning from hers. I never knew when my eyes got closed, but in few seconds they got open again expressing dissatisfaction of what it saw. By now she walked gently without being shy with Dooshima to her seat. Tranquility was on the throne. It was surprising how a young lady's presence could bring silence more than our teachers. The boys could not keep an eye off her, they were all quiet just staring at her. We were quiet that someone could easily detect the movement of an ant in our midst. I was astonished seeing such a beautiful lady. I could not stop staring at her as well, since Dooshima's desk was directly beside me on the third row. When she tried turning at my side I would avert my eyes immediately and pretend to be reading. I had not felt like this before. My mates thought I had no feelings for the ladies. I was also surprised about what happened. Some of my troublesome female mates were laughing at me as they saw my expression. The boys had no cause to laugh back at me because they had also taken their share. She was busy talking with Dooshima. I believe she knew what was going on, but she showed no concern. I would open and close and open back my note book staring as though I was reading. But not a single thing had I comprehended in the process. It amused me greatly when I later discovered I was counting lines instead of reading. I was counting over and over in the same paragraph but this was not the right time for me to make an attempt to fuss out laughter. She and Dooshima discussed for some minutes and later on they stood and left the class. Our female mates burst into laughter immediately the lady and Dooshima had left the class. Some of them were patient enough and they started hailing me –Pastor De Pastor… without waiting on me to explain to them. Frankly I did not hold any explanation on what went on, could I even help myself understand it not to talk of explaining or forcing to be okay in the presence of my mates. The class was so noisy, yet the voices of my mates who crowded me were heard as they were shouting at me T.K the lover boy… T.K the lover boy… So motionless I sat back only smiling at them, as though I never gave a damn but deep in my mind I was already plotting graph on how to get the intercept. Dooshima was not going to escape a single question from me anytime she comes back in the class as I was going to ask –ask her many questions. She was going to tell me whether it was her sister or perhaps a friend either. I was never expecting it to be her brother's friend at all. Not only me, she was going to answer many questions from my mates as well. I felt weak as she announced to my ears on our way home that she was meeting her for the first time. And that it was the mother of the lady, Mrs. Ikyaagba, one of our teachers who teaches Christian Religious Knowledge in the Junior classes that introduced her daughter to her. Dooshima told me that she came to register SSCE with us. She said, the lady had already graduated from secondary school but she had an issue in Mathematics which prevented her from gaining admission into the university. Dooshima had finally killed me when she said the lady seemed cheeky, that she claimed not to be sorghum for every fowl. She said the lady had indirectly let her to know that she was not of our class, which she claimed to know what we were all doing on her arrival. Well, I said in my heart after Dooshima had said all these. After all it is the desire of a dog to sleep in ashes and not because of the burnt hut. Really it was not because of what Dooshima had said but rather I gave an expression to show that I heard what she said. My poor background coupled with my mum's words were what made not even think of approaching her.

II

After the exams we did not meet till it was after my graduation that we met again. When I was coming back from work one evening, I branched to a big shopping plaza in town to buy some items for my mum then I met her. She also came to get some items. She had been there before me. I did not notice her presence when I walked in hence the plaza was very big, immediately I finished shopping and began to push my items to the cashier's table, I heard a voice that sounded as though it was coming from my heart. Another count I was barely declaring that I heard an angel questioning me. 'Hello! Is it not T.K?' when I lifted up my eyes I saw a pretty lady who was at the cashier's table looking right at me. The face looked acquainted, I said it in heart. But I hardly got the image straight. It was as I moved closer that I clearly recognized her, I was surprised to see her again in my life. She had now fully grown into a woman more beautiful than before. She was surprised as well. I confidently approached her with a hand shake allowing my cheeks to draw back showing a long-time-no-see smiles without hesitation. She also responded with a radiant smile that made my emotions of years back ride into my heart, instantly making my body to feel warm and joyous like a baby in the coddling hands of the mother in a cold weather. I could believe now was more of maturity. 'Waoh! You are right it's me T.K. It has been a long time, you have a good memory I must compliment,' I evenly said. 'Thanks, I must confess I can't just forget your giant structure, not even when your face is covered.' She said and had me put in the wings of my ego with her compliment. 'Waoh! You amazed me so much, how are you doing?' 'Fine, I'm good,' she said smartly. 'I can see it's obvious you look more magnifi…' 'Don't go there,' she interrupted delightedly. 'Alright, I can see you are already through with your shopping' 'Exactly, I suppose and you?' 'Ehm yea, so what are you up to?' 'I have to get home now,' she said and turned to the cashier to collect her balance and I made some sign for the cashier to give back what she paid but she sensed it and refused and I had to say, 'don't worry I will pay for you' but rather she declined saying, 'thank you don't worry too…' 'No come-on, it is an offer, don't tell me you want to rebuff my offer just like that' 'Sorry don't bother, thank you, I have to leave, maybe some other time' 'Alright, it's ok' I said accepting her refusal. I paid for my items and moved out with her in one shadow. 'Can I give you a lift' I demanded very calmly. 'No' she sounded hesitantly but I insisted and finally she accepted. I was too open in my talk to her on the way that she could not get long to open up as well. In dribs we talked about ourselves after our pass out from the secondary school and we finally exchange our phone contacts. Some days after we started having dinners, by my persistence and we later fell in love. That was how we got married. We were happily married, I loved her so much and I promised to love her all the rest of my life. I could remember that day of our wedding. I could remember what I did on our wedding day. I could remember the words I whispered to her ears after we had taken our vows, after I had kissed my wife as it is conventional. Articulating that I was now a man, I then let my palms cover her cheeks. I looked into her eyes with passion, people's eyes were expressing surprise, it seemed to be strange to them as to what I intend doing. Some eyes were already drawing conclusion that I wasn't satisfied with the kiss, and I bent forward, on a final note. They hoped another kiss from me but to their utmost surprise I turned my head sideways as though I was placing my cheek at her left shoulder. Rather, my mouth quivered and opened, and I whispered into her ears, 'Iveren, today we have been proclaimed as husband and wife, I truly love you, I promise I will not hurt you, I will not let your eyes shade tears, I will care for you, be with you all the days of my life. I promise to be to you like a father, I promise to be to you like a brother, but promise me you will not hurt me and you will remain a good and God fearing woman all your life.' I felt like I was the only man standing when she whispered back into my ears. 'I promise you my heart; I will not leave you, as my heart beat so my love for you will be, endless as long as I live.' I was indeed full with joy that the guests without hearing our conversation began clapping in excitement.

III

Life was going smoothly. I and my wife were so united. It made my mum and siblings very happy. Since that was something to make my mum and siblings very happy I was ever ready to make them happier. It wasn't what they would expect from me after all they had gone through. I had made effort so much to make my mother and siblings hold the wings and horns of happiness, they so much deserved love from me. They deserved comfort and I was glad to be giving them in its fullness. They were the reason why I married my loving wife Iveren, they deserved everything from me and I would never relent in supporting them till the last drop of my blood. My siblings had stopped schooling when they were in the junior secondary school just to put me through the higher institution for six complete years. I will never forget what they went through to make me a better person after our father sent us away and married another wife. I will never forget that day for the rest of my life. I was 16 years old then, my siblings, Terdoo was 11 and Doom was 7 years old. That wicked day, it had happened after rainy season in the month of November. We had harvested all our farm produce with the exception of sorghum and cassava that we were still uprooting to pill and dry so as to make tapioca. Our farm produce were amazing to look at, no one had ever thought that our crops would yield like that. That very year, we had got two thousand tubers of yam and they were stored at home. Our beni seed was also threshed and packaged into 6 bags, groundnut had been sold 7 bags and 10 were left in the store, our soybeans was also threshed and stored in 10 bags. It was a surprise to people of the village how our soybeans was harvested earlier than others, although it was an improved variety. They did not notice that their varieties were local ones compared to ours. Some had been gossiping that it was charms that my mother had been using in her farm. And some would come to her with another ideology that it is her hands that were filled with such good luck so she should be the one to start their seasonal operations. My mother was a wise woman. She had finished from upper class before she married my father. She was a very hardworking woman. Many people in our village had wished they were the ones who had married such a woman. And with such mindset, envy and jealousy set in. But that was not a grateful thing in the sight of my father. We had then enough to eat. My father was a trader, he had no passion for farm work. He hated going to the farm, but he was the one in charge of the farm produce. He would only help my mother with farm hands and after tillage, the rest would be the responsibility of my mother. He would visit the farm only when the crops were up to harvest to check how it might count in bags. He started doing that the very time he married my mother. Our mother would be in the farm alone till we were born and grew up to start working with her. That Friday we went to the farm with our mother very early as we had planned the previous night before we went to bed. We had arranged that the next day we would uproot and dry all the remaining cassava in the yam farm. We had made efforts to finish it, but it was very late. We reached home after four in the evening. What had delayed our return home much was the packaging of the already dried ones into bags so as to push them back home and store for consumption in the period of June, July and August when yams would be scarce. I pushed the cassava in the truck with Terdoo to the store. Terdoo went to the room to pick the store keys. My mum had dropped down her load of firewood and pawpaw with some vegetable leaves that were to be prepared that night. While Doom took a stainless steel bowl with plates and an empty jerry-can that we took drinking water to the farm with. Her load was not much because of how far the house was with the farm. My mother quickly stormed into the kitchen and started connecting firewood together to make fire, so that she would prepare food for us. As Terdoo had gone to bring the store keys, I noticed some tyre lines of a vehicle, from the store to a street in front of our house that led to the major road of the village. I was confused but I said nothing and no other had observed it. When Terdoo brought the store keys we were all flabbergasted, we all shouted 'Jesus' at once, the muscles of my mouth refused to shut the mouth up because of what the eyes had seen and informed it. Our mother expressed shock from the kitchen, and the knife she was pilling yam with fell down immediately. She rushed out because of the loud shriek that echoed in her ears. I stood transfixed. It was Terdoo who had run to our mother to announce what we had seen. 'Wana, ka nyi?' our mother asked Terdoo what was the matter as he ran to her. 'Mama Thieves have broken in and emptied our store, nothing is left,' Terdoo explained furiously. But now our mother was rather calm in her conversation. I was so surprised with the question she asked, that did we meet the store open when we came back? I had thought this was what our mother would dash herself on the ground and start weeping but she didn't. It made me to have a rethink. She had now noticed the sign of the vehicle tyre, she stared suspiciously around the compound. She said nothing and then she turned back to the kitchen, and we were all confused how our mother had acted on such a case without anxiety. It seemed she knew something about it. We began rushing to the kitchen to find out. Many question we had asked our mother but she said nothing, rather she asked us to go and take our baths. We disturbed her but she said nothing, rather she asked whether she had not gone to the farm with us? We felt weak and then walked out of the kitchen leaving her with Doom to take our bath as she demanded. We took our bath and a little later our mother finished preparing 'luam' of pounded yam and vegetable leaves with fish, but we had all lost our appetite. We only ate little so as not to starve. Terdoo and Doom slept, but I was unable to sleep till the time clocked 11:00pm. I hardly recall when I drifted off to later hear someone screaming in my dream. I jerked up and discovered it was real, my mother was the one screaming. I rushed into the bedroom. I was really mad when I saw my father whipping my mother thoroughly like a horse with his belt. Whipping hardly and fast like the running of the seconds hand of a clock. She was injured on several parts of her body and was seriously bleeding. I became a man in a split of some seconds. Up till today I have never understood how I ran and got hold of my father's belt. It was so mysterious as little as I was as to how giant my father was. He was very strong, if he got hold of you, you always regret why you were conceived. My mother ran out and then my father got hold of me. But my savior was our neighbor, Mama Bunde. She was a widow. She heard cries rising greatly from our household and she rushed into our housing thinking we had lost someone. But before she arrived, my father had divided my left ear with the head of his belt. Indeed we cried as though we lost someone but it was my father who was the bone of contention. After rescuing me, Mama Bunde approached my father to calm him down and settle the matter but rather my father asked her to get out of his house calling her –chief Judge of the federation. He went to the backyard and took a stick and was coming over to where my mother sat weeping. On seeing him, my mother ran out of the house to Mama Bunde's house. We also ran over and met her. Our father threatened us never to come back to his house, that death would be the result. I was startled when I heard from my mother the reason of what had happened. That it was because she confronted him for emptying the store. I sought but nature could not give me what my father was made of. My father was a very wicked man. I wondered why he was doing all these. Mama Bunde was not astonished, rather she got into the kitchen and prepared hot water. She pressed on my mother's wounds and also on my left ear and robbed our affected parts with her balm. It was now that I recalled and came to conformity with what Mama Bunde had told me one day when I was at home playing football in the field at the back of our house with my peer group. I felt angry with her because of the interruption, I never wanted to go but when I thought of her kindness, how she used to be with my mother then I decided to go. She held my hand. 'Waneô' how are you today?' 'Mama I am fine,' I replied. I thought she wanted to send me at first but now she was taking me to her hut. 'T.K wan wan ma, why didn't you go to the farm today?' she asked me immediately we entered the hut. I felt guilt and could not answer her, and she repeated again and I said nothing. Then she pointed at a wooden stool in the hut and asked me to sit down and I sat down. She stared at me like a mother on her child. She smiled at me and asked me again. 'Ordedoo, why didn't you go to farm with your mother and siblings?' Now, I was compelled to answer her. Her warm mother-like words and smiles that were so bright on her face were the cause of it. 'Mama nothing' I said thoughtlessly. 'Nothing but why did you just decide not to follow your mother and siblings to the farm?' I remain silent with my head tilted looking down my feet and in some seconds she summoned back. 'See let me tell you, you are an obedient child, everyone in this village knows it. It is because of your obedience and honesty that I love you so much if you don't know. The eyes of your mother's enemies are seeing and they are beginning to rejoice because of the sudden change of your attitude. They don't want anything good from your mother. They would have done some evil things to your mother because of how hardworking she was, because of how determined she is, because of the great reputation she has for being with a man like your father, for how generous she is. But they had no cause of guilt on her. You see, they are always happy with the attitude your father portrays towards your mother. Please my son do not disgrace your mother but rather her enemies. Obey her and don't change from your assiduousness, be ready to support your mother and you will receive blessings from God and prosper. Don't make your mother regret why she conceived you. You are the eldest one, our people would say; the straightness of a road is from the starting. That is why it is the first man on a journey in the night that puts on the light. So it is how you go your little siblings will follow and if you direct them in a wrong way your mother will become a laughing stock in this village. How lonely she would be, no good husband to keep company and even her children? Please my son, I beg of you consider how your mother suffered before giving birth to you. Please don't renew the wounds your father had caused. See, when you were yet to be born and were still in your mother's womb, your father would go somewhere and return in the middle of the night and again command your mother to cook another food for him with her pregnancy. He would beat your mother like a slave. He would sell all that your mother had worked for. Your mother had suffered much from your father's hands but she would tell no one, only I had known, because her grandmother and my mother were from the same village. I keep on telling her to continue with her endurance. But all these, your father was never grateful. So please my son don't be obstinate. If your mother comes back, go and beg her to forgive you for what you have done.' After she said this I went out guiltily and henceforth I repented from what I did, for the story really touched me but I wonder how I got to forget it so quickly as not to take remembrance of it when I first discovered the empty store. The next day we did not know what to do, after all our father had declared that we should not return back to the house. Mama Bunde told my mother to send for her people since our father was still abrasive. We slept in Mama Bunde's house for two days before two of my mother's uncles came. They arrived in the afternoon while my father was not around so they waited for him till he later came back in the evening. We went with our mother's uncles including Mama Bunde so that my mother's uncles would settle the matter but to every ones utmost surprise he refused to attend to them. He ignored them, took his bath left them in the house with words that, 'ne tuma a kuma ne tso ne mough ne yem hen u yar enev,' meaning when they are tired of seating they would return back to their homes. We decided to come back to Mama Bunde's house. Later in the night my mother's uncles discussed and finally agreed on taking us away.

IV

Indeed situations would make one understand wise saying clearer. It was now that I knew the meaning of, from frying pan to fire. This was indeed from frying pan to fire. Staying with my siblings and my mother in her village was like Jonah in the belly of a fish, like a blind man thrown in a pit, it was not easy. My mother had no siblings, she was just alone, and her mother could not give birth again after her. Her parents loved her so much. Even as they were poor, living and depending on farming, they valued education so much. They promised to give her sound education, and had tried to the level of Form Five. Unfortunately, it was on the day of her final paper that her parents all died in a ghastly motor accident on their way to one of their relative's funeral ceremony. She could not further her education, when her uncle, her father's immediate younger brother, who inherited all her father's property had refused to sponsor her. She became to them like a slave. She suffered much under their care and as she could no longer bear it, she then married to my father who had promised to take care of her education. But the reverse became the case which had driven her to a phase of a mysterious life. In my mother's house, we were staying with my mother's uncle, Mhonom who with his cousins had taken us back. He was the last born out of the three in their family. He gave us two of his rooms to be staying in. He was a kind man but his wife was otherwise, a wolf in sheep clothing. We did not know where to begin. But Mhonom accepted to take care of us since we had nothing to take care of ourselves with. For we had taken nothing out with the exception of our wears that our father had thrown out that night. Uncle Mhonom's wife, Yuhwe expressed grievances toward what her husband had said. She was not comfortable over my mother's coming back to stay with them. After four months, the rainy season started and propitiously Mama Bunde visited us. She brought for us a half bag of groundnut seeds, a sack of soybeans and some cups of sorghum and millet. Uncle Mhonom gave our mother parcels of land to cultivate. He also invited the village youth to help our mother get some ridges and hills so she could plant some little crops and many accepted. They made enough ridges and hills for my mother. We also cultivated cassava and the yam seeds that some women in the village gave my mother, in addition to all that Mama Bunde had given us. The first year, we had harvested enough to take care of ourselves and not to depend on Uncle Mhonom again. Our mother sold some of the farm product and used the money to for our admission. Terdoo and I were admitted in the same secondary school while Doom was admitted in a primary school that was in the village in primary five, Terdoo was then in JSS2 while I was in SSS2. Our school was far from our mother's village. Since within the village there was no secondary school, we would trek from our house to school and trek back every day. The next year our farm products were much better than the previous year and we were very happy. I was now in SSS3 so my mother gathered some farm produce and sold to register my Senior School Certificate Examination (SSCE). What a coincidence that year, I was registering external examination, Terdoo was in JSS3 and was to be registered for Junior School Certificate Examination (JSCE) and Doom was to write common entrance exam into secondary school. Uncle Mhonom's wife was not happy for us, our progress she had never liked it, whenever we smiled it offended her. She had married him for 9 years but had not given birth to a single child. Not too long she started having problems with my mother. She hated us without reason of our guilt and every day she would find fault in my mother and would insult her and throw a lot of provocative utterances. My mother would endure untill one day she became tired of it and reported to her husband. He was very angry that such a thing had been happening and my mother had not told him. He expressed great annoyance over it and apologized, promising my mother that it won't happen again. Afterward Mhonom expressed dislike to his wife over what she had been doing and his wife refused to comply with his orders and it became another problem between the two of them. So my mother called Mhonom and told him that they were living together without problems but since her staying with them has brought problems she would not stay with them again. She said she did not want to become marriage breaker, igniting fire in peoples unions so he should take some of the money she sold her farm produce and make thatch houses for her to live with her children. He refused not to let it happen that a woman cannot pursue his sister away from his house but my mother insisted. Few weeks we all packed into our new house, and were now living alone. Ever since we started harvesting bountifully, many people in the village became envious and unhappy but it wasn't known to us. It was as it reached the state of some even rejecting our greetings on walk paths on our way to the farm and market and even in the church that we understood clearly how serious it was.

They had never wanted us not to progress but turn to beggars, so that we become objects of ridicule in the village. Our very hardworking disposition really irritated them. Some had one day murmured it out in the stream that our obsession for work and focus to achieve made them hate us with passion. The third year we planted more than the other years and we did not know what had happened to our farm. All our crops withered just like that as though there was no moisture. We did not understand why it was so. We had nothing to harvest that year. Things turned aback for us. and even to eat became a problem. My mother decided to start selling fried yams in the village market. That was the little thing that was now putting food on our table. Although it was not all that lucrative but she sought to do it so she could take care of us. My mother managed and bought some crops and cultivated again but it was now even worse than the other year. She finally decided to continue with her yam business. She struggled and made way to register Joint Admission and Matriculation (JAMB) for me and by God's grace, I scored it well. In as much as how hard it was my mother had been putting more effort in her yam business to meet our needs. But all of a sudden the yam business also started crumbling. At times she would fry yam and no one would ever ask her how much for it. But she refused to give up. I and my siblings would go to people's farm to work for them to get some money to enable our mother. We would also go to work in building sites. Our mother would not be happy with it but we would insist to help as we could. That was how we were striving to survive. One Friday in the evening we were all at home our mother had just returned from the market. She sat in the kitchen and was removing the things she bought to prepare the meal for the day and I was standing at the kitchen door with Terdoo while Doom was also in the kitchen when my friend whom we wrote JAMB together came with the news that I was offered admission into University of Nigeria, Nsukka to study medicine and surgery. It came to us like a storm, we were very happy. The joy that came in was so great, I felt like flying only that I had no wings. My siblings were already jumping into the sky if not for the force of gravity, they would have made way to hang into the sky and my mother on the other side was dancing like never before. I held the letter and was just looking at my name and the content with a smile imagining myself working on patients in the hospital as a doctor. I felt like a one-day governor. All of a sudden my mother stopped dancing and her countenance changed. What I saw next I could not believe it, great tears were dripping down her cheeks. She sighed heavily and more tears started rushing out like that of the intense pressure of water out of a pipe. I became dumbfounded. My siblings went on demanding what the matter was all about. My mother wailed and wailed and she began to lament, 'God where are you? Poor woman like me how can I train my children? Who would I run to? Would this opportunity still pass my son? Look at my condition oh God in heaven.' The joy died and we all became moody with our mother's lamentation. She wept throughout the night. Days were moving gradually but we had nothing to keep for a single payment till a week after the date set for resumption. I and my siblings were working in the site and the contractor came around. He saw us and asked some of the senior workers why they allowed little children like my siblings to do such work but he was told that it was us who insisted that we could do it. He became compassionate and interested in us. He sat me down and demanded to know about us when he was told that we were of the same blood. I told him all the story of our life, before I would finish I had rained my cheeks with tears severally. I was shocked when I saw the man dabbing his eyes with handkerchief. He was greatly gripped by the wind of the horrific story. He asked my siblings to stop work. He followed us home that very day. He spoke with my mother and told her that he would take care of my responsibility till I graduate from the university. Before he ended his statement my mother fell on her knees thanking him with ceaseless tears. We all knelt down to thank him. He seized my mum and raised her to her feet and told her not to weep again. He also told us to stand up and stop crying but this was not that easy for my mother. She cried a lot upon realizing that all the misfortune descended down and clung unto her heavy heart. She wailed greatly even as she promised the man not to, after he had left to return for us the next day.

V

With great sympathy he returned back the next day. We were so happy. We lack words of gratitude to give. His full name was Oryiman Ma'Quin. His life style entailed that he was an honest man. He asked me to prepare so that we would go to the school and find out all that was to be done. I quickly rushed into the bathroom. I can possibly count the seconds that I used in the bathroom that day as a result of the joy that was whirling inside of me. Before my mother would ask whether I had gone to the bathroom, I had already finished dressing up, I quickly gathered my documents and enclosed them into a brown colored envelope and clutched it in my armpit and my shuttle bag on the right hand side, looking like an old village headmaster as I came out of the room. Everyone was astonished how swift I had been and without waste of time, we set off. The happiest thing that I had ever experienced was when I entered the university gate, the lion's den as they would call it, which was all by the favor of a man I had not known. What wasn't desired by my biological father to do for me, but another man wearing his responsibility as though he was dead or we had something in common with him. With this, even as I entered the gate of the university happily, the pains were so great that my chest swelled up. My heart became dried that it drained up all the glands within my throat making it stiff and dried as well. Analyzing that there was a call for tears as all the misfortune of our life fell back into my mind as a result of our father negligence. I survived stopping the flow of the tears, instead I made it hung around my eye balls so as to assert maturity in sir Oryiman's presence. It was already 12pm when we arrived. He swerved through some streets in the school and finally alighted in front of one complex with a very bold inscription in blue 'ACADEMIC BLOCK'. He collected my envelope and asked me to follow him. I was just moving with him from one office to another. Many persons knew him. They were greeting him with his name in every office we walked in. It seemed as though it was his alma-mater a. I knew nothing about what was happening. I was only under instruction, sit down and take passport and I will sit, press and hold your thumb and I will do it. My first time in such an environment, made me scared as it was strange to me. I nearly hands akimbo with my mouth open like my village relatives did when they first saw cinema in our village market. I had to show difference at least as a more literate person and remove all doubt, since my appearance could not explain. We processed a lot but could not finish it that day. Sir Oryiman lodged two rooms for us in one hotel outside the school gate. It was in the evening when we returned to the hotel that he explained some of the processes that we had done to me. He finally told me that, that was the institution he graduated from. He also told me how stressful and annoying it would have been if at all he allowed me to come alone, telling me about some people that I saw outside of the school gate in canopies. He said that they were also new intakes undergoing the same process. He said since he had many of the staff as his friends he ought not to stress himself out there in the canopies. I was very grateful, we ate that night and slept. The next day, we went back to the school. Before 11:00am, I was surprised when we came out of one office of the hostel administrators telling me that he had finished everything. That the only thing left was for me to come back home and park my things for school. A heavy storm of joy engulfed me and I jumped and hugged him with a lot of thank you sir. I was so happy that our coming back home was to me like days' journey. I was longing to break the news to my mum and siblings. At least I had learnt something from the students within the two days. They would call a male student, lion and call a female student, lioness and the institution itself den. I had gotten an ascribed nick name that my siblings would be hailing me with. It was not little jubilation when we finally arrived home. My mother prepared pounded yam with fluted pumpkin leaves under the meat umbrella of a chicken. I was surprised as to where she got it considering our condition. After the meal Oryiman gave my mother the sum of N40, 000 to get me the necessary things so that in two days he would take me back to school. At the moment we were the only happiest people on earth. It seemed as though it was a dream but it was reality. Like joke I truly became a lion in the den hunting not for lionesses but what really took me into the den, which was knowledge, hunting it with a great determination to achieve and as well not to let the knees that supports me get disappointed. Life on campus was like men in the jungle, socially abbreviated as OYO, meaning On Your Own. But to God, Oryiman had been meeting all my needs, whenever I called on him.

It had been long now in the second semester in my year two. I decided not to bother him since I could endure with the condition and finish up the semester exams before I come back home yearning to become a 300 level student so quickly. I came back home as a lion in no more two steps but three steps, I slept the night and the next day I and my mother left the house to greet Oryiman as we normally do whenever I am back for a break and also tell him about my experience this time. His house was in the town that I had gone to secondary school which was called Gboko while my mother's village was Kucha. When we were proximal to the house, the smell of the house was not familiar and it did not appeal to my liking. Another strange thing was that the gate of the house was wide open. I and my mother stopped a little at the corner of the gate to see whether it was a car that was about to go out but we heard no sound and then we marched inside the house. We saw Oryiman's wife squatting on the ground in the front of the house with many people circling her, we hastened our feet to where they were and immediately as his wife saw me, she shrieked out in tears but it had seemed she cried for so long that what I heard was only my name. When we fully met them my mother quickly demanded from them what was the matter. What I could remember last after I had revived was what the women said when my mother demanded from them, that Oryiman is dead. I revived to see my mother at my right still unconscious. We spent three days in the hospital before we finally recovered. How painful it was but we had no power to bring him back to life. Hopelessly, we watched him buried. Now I understood again the proverb that say, nearest does not kill a bird. We were now left on our own feet to continue with our cross. After a month school resumed and I was to go back. That was where money took it, hindering the way. My mother managed and gave me transport fare with some foodstuff to resume hoping that I will pay part of my fees in the next three weeks after they had finished the contract of weeding someone's yam and groundnut farms. But when I reached school and started lectures it came hard that I had to buy some of my personal practical materials for practicals and some compulsory textbooks, which cost was over twenty thousand naira and without the items there was no way for me to carryout practicals and that alone was covering about 40% of assessment in totality. I decided to return back home and explain everything to my mother. I talked to her and without any other effort to make, she accepted my opinion of going back to school to defer my admission. I went back and met one of Oryiman's friends in one of the offices we visited during my admission process. After we had finished the process I returned back home but things were not favorable. So with my mother permission, although she was very scared allowing me to go to Makurdi, but it was for betterment. I went and dwelt with my friend where I started working with him for TTB as a conductor and my friend a driver moving from Wurukun to North bank, from North bank to Wadata, from Wadata to Modern market, from Modern market to high level, from High level to Brewery and Gaadi routes. That was where and how I worked for a whole year and got money for the next session, my mates were going into 400 level while I was coming into 300 level. It was as Oryiman was now no more that I understood what students would say, school no easy, but mine was like a different one. It was like an integration of many 'no easy,' for my experience was too rough. For a poor child to be reading medicine and surgery in the university was never a simple task. I would have to go beyond expectation only not to disappoint my lovely mother. Sometimes I wondered what my teachers meant when they would say the hardest stage of school is the secondary school. With my sufferings, there was no single reason for me to accept their opinion, not even in my next world. It was the university that made me understood what people would say that school is not meant for the poor, and it is the fact. In the same year three second semester I had a challenge of money again. I had to follow a very big van that was coming to Gboko, the man who was a driver accepted helping me I had waited for such opportunity coming to the van garage for three days so I could have my way home and find some foodstuff and money for photocopying of materials. I was very happy as I finally fell in the hands of that kind man. But things were very difficult at home as usual, the only money left at home I was told that they treated Terdoo's snake bite with it when he went to work with Doom in one man's farm so as to get some money for me. My mother was also ill. I cried and wished to have not been given birth. My mother wiped my tears and told me not to cry anymore and stop saying those words, that the one who created me is still alive. And that he was the one who permitted that I should fall in the hands of Oryinman and he is the one who took him away. That all things belonged to him, and I should only glorify him. I was startled when I heard those words from my mother. I wondered whether they were coming exactly from her, for the mother I know weeps greatly over every critical situations, but how come the preaching. I persistently asked her what had transpired during my absence and was finally told that she had come to know the power of the Lord we serve under the umbrella of Catholic Charismatic Renewal. So I should not bother all will be well. My mother sold some of her wrappers and even her only remaining beautiful sandals and gave me money to go back and I shamelessly collected the money for I had nothing to do. The rest of my staying in school was not easy after Oryiman's death. Whenever on holidays I would go back to Makurdi to do bus conductor and gather some little money and couple with the one my mother and siblings would work and keep for me. My siblings had really suffered for me I had caused then great pain. Oh yes my mother was a very lovely mother. God had done a great thing to have given us such a mother.

Many times I wondered how life on earth would have been without her. She was too good by my description. I had realized that, when David in the bible wrote about a virtues woman he was actually talking about my mother.

VI

Looking all at what I, my mother and siblings had gone through because of my father I had then promised my life time not to measure my father's steps. Not to let my children have such a story in their life and not my wife as well face a misfortune life. So I allowed my love blow everywhere like wind. I had great affection on my family. I cherished my wife with passion as it pleased my mother, hence it gave my mother great joy. I was ever ready to keep to my promises. My mother had trained me well in every aspect to be a real man. But in the long run, my wife took it opportunity to be timidity. She started nagging when work became too much for me. I would go to work some times and return late at night and when I explained to my wife, she would refuse to listen to me. Her thoughts were only that I was cheating on her. She would quarrel and say many things that I used to close from work early and hang out with my secret lovers, claiming to be a hardworking man. She continued till I decided to start hanging out, even whenever I closed early thinking it would bring peace of mind. It kept occurring like that. I was always keeping quiet to all her problems for I had tasted the end point of such things. Not too long my friends started calling me and telling me things about my wife. Some were texting me on phone. But I answered no one. I loved my wife and I needed no third party in our union. I never allowed my wife's nagging to crave way for problem in our marriage and not to create room for friends to destroy our marriage. I had known much about what happened in some marriages as a result of friends reporting to one about his or her partner. So I refused to be part and parcel of it. I nearly had a problem with one of my friends one day. He called me during working hours and was telling me to go to a certain hotel and see things myself. One fateful Wednesday I had to travel to far north precisely in Kano, on a medical check. A good friend of mine had a cardiovascular disease. The last time I visited him, I did some medical work on him and he was seriously relieved from the illness. It was over four years. But last two days he called me and was telling me that he wanted to see me urgently that the problem was up again. So I had to go and check on him. Very early I took my two kids to school and from there I set off. I had to spend more than a day. So I had to carry my briefcase along. Nothing had been hidden to my wife as she waved us out on the street. On my way, my car tyre had been a roadside fan to other cars. I rode very fast. I had reached the state already but the town was quite a little distance. Not too long I had a call. It was from the family of my friend telling me that he had given up. It was very terrible, I was shocked. It touched me greatly. I felt pains all over my body. I could not drive at that moment so I had to park by the roadside for a while. Ever since I was a medical doctor I had not felt like that for a patient not because he was my friend but the circumstance at hand. Later on, I arrived at the house. I met his wife and his daughter. His two sons had just taken him to the hospital and I quickly rushed to the hospital with her daughter before he was taken to the mortuary. And we all returned back there after. I gave words of consolation and prayed with them and I told them that I would visit them before the burial. I decided to go back home. I reached Makurdi late. It was getting to 9 O'clock in the night but I never wanted to sleep in Makurdi where my mother and siblings were, so I decided to go back to Gboko since I was having some other issues in my hospital to handle. Fortunately for me, I entered the town before I had a punched tyre so I decided to park the car and take a bike I was grateful for them working at late hours at least they had helped my soul. The bike man rode gently and cautiously and I alighted at the gate of my house, because of it I paid him more than the stipulated amount. At least I was back home to have a good rest after the stress. I knocked on my gate and my gateman quickly opened the gate, after seeing me through the check hole. It seemed he had not yet slept. I walked in and as I was heading to the flat, I had a turn back and I saw him holding his head with his two hands and moving to his room. Perhaps he had thought to be lucky as not to leave for home in my absence as I had earlier warned. I winked and shook my head as I kept moving toward the door. I was surprised as the door was not locked, for I presumed that they might have slept. I walked in full of stress, the weather was very cold, I had to walk up stairs so that I would have my bath, I had pull off my suit already. As I approached my bedroom door, I heard some pleasurable scream and I got hold of the knob on the door, when I opened the door my eyes saw what my mouth could not shout. I was shocked. At first I thought it was a dream but it wasn't. In real life I saw a man descending heavily on my wife in my matrimonial home on my matrimonial bed like a stone under the force of gravity. Yes indeed my mouth had seen what my eyes could not say. All of a sudden my body temperature changed. Perspiration started gathering over my brow. There was sweat all over my body in such inclement. Their eyes then sighted me and they abruptly stood. I was surprised when I discovered myself counting within me. I had now counted up to thirty as my mother had thought me to do so whenever I felt bad over something. By now the chemistry within me had produced silence and I said nothing. Instead, I closed back the door and walked back to my sitting room. Even after everything, I had said nothing. I knew not how the man made his way out of my house and I also placed no concern. I spoke with her normally as husband and wife but I said nothing about what had happened. I slept in my sitting room that night. Even as the day broke, I was still normal. I took the kids to school and back to work. For two days, I said nothing, did nothing, neither pondered over what had happened. On the third day I went to work as normal and came back home to meet only the kids with my gate man, I asked him where my wife had gone to but he told me that he had no idea about it. I called her line but it was not going through. She did not come home till the next day. I still left for work as usual but returned home early so as to take the kids back home. I called my mother and asked her whether my wife visited her but she said she didn't see her. I went to my wife's house. That was the first thing I did the next day, where my wife's parents were living in the town with their entire family. I was so fortunate that I met everyone at home. My wife had two brothers and a sister who had already married. They were four in the family. My wife was the first child of her parents. Her sister Mlumum that had married followed and then her two brothers. My father in-law and my in-laws were all in the sitting room while my wife and her mother were in another room. Immediately as I walked in everywhere became quiet. I genuflected as I greeted them but it was only my father in-law that answered. The two of my wife's brothers ignored my greetings disdainfully. My father in-law was a good man. He loved me so much. In a while with them I requested to see and greet my mother in-law and I moved to where she was. My wife was startled when she saw me. I greeted them, but my mother in-law responded in a weak manner and my wife did not respond at all. I said some words with my mother in-law and then came back to the sitting room. It seemed my in-laws were out. It was only my father in-law that was now in the sitting room. It was not too long before my in-laws came back to the sitting room with some guys looking like thugs. They were breathing heavily and then my in-laws pointed at me saying this is the man. Immediately the guys pulled out a whip made of animal skin from their back and approached me very terribly. And they added after teaching him a lesson take him out and decide what you want on him. At once their father shouted and told the guys not to try it if at all they love their lives. And then they held their actions, my wife and her mother then rushed out to the sitting room. And my father in-law continued, 'What nonsense is this, are you two mad? Has it gone to this level? You never try this kind of thing in my presence. Have you heard his version of what happened? You only heard from your sister and you want to crucify him, no… no… that won't happen when I'm alive. Not at all. You must be silly I won't accept that." I was perplexed, just staring at them as they were also looking at me furiously. My father in-law asked me 'My son what is the matter with you and your wife? Why is your wife back home?' 'Daddy I am sorry I did not have any misunderstanding with my wife. I had not seen her and I thought she would be here, that is why I came over. If only she said there is a problem then I will also like to hear from her what it is.' After I had said this, my father in-law turned to his daughter to ask her whether she heard me and lo her eyes were pumping tears down her cheeks, she quickly ran out of the sitting room and her mother followed her. After on, I went to where they were. Immediately my mother in-law saw me she fell on my knees and busted into tears. I raised her up. 'Mama, what is the matter? Why are you crying?' I asked but she was still crying. 'Mama I told you that there is no problem but why are you still crying?' 'My son, your wife had told me everything, hai! I am finished. I am finished.' She began to cry again. My wife was also rolling in tears on the ground. I raised both of them and asked them to stop crying. 'Mama everything is over. I have forgiven her that is why am here to take her back.' 'My son, I am eternally indebted. I have not seen a man like you ever in my life. My son let heavens rain on you all the days of your life. I am sorry for what your in-laws did to you. I must have them apologize to you. Please forgive them too my son, I don't know what to…' 'Mama, it is fine. I didn't come over to have a verbal recap of what had happened so please mama forget about it,' I said interruptedly. My in-laws felt shame and sorry for they. They render apologies and we took off. I brought my wife back and today I am happy to tell you that there is no difference between mother-Mary and her. She had set a covenant with the Lord as not to see another man again. Thus I owe you words that; it is not every situation that deserve cruel actions but instead key into silence and watch as things will fall on your feet.

ABOUT THE AUTHOR

Mparegh Bernard Mveuter is a young trained forester,

who has flair for writing. He lives in Gboko, Benue Nigeria. The flow of ashes and virtue of silence is his first attempt at writting.

www.ingramcontent.com/pod-product-compliance
Lightning Source LLC
LaVergne TN
LVHW041118150826
845673LV00007B/2109